MILDRED'S
MARRIED LIFE

The Original Mildred Classics

Mildred Keith

Mildred at Roselands

Mildred and Elsie

Mildred's Married Life

Mildred at Home

Mildred's Boys and Girls

Mildred's New Daughter

MILDRED'S
MARRIED LIFE

Book Four of
The Original Mildred Classics

MARTHA FINLEY

CUMBERLAND HOUSE
NASHVILLE, TENNESSEE

MILDRED'S MARRIED LIFE
by Martha Finley

Any unique characteristics of this edition:
Copyright (c) 2001 by Cumberland House Publishing, Inc.

Published by Cumberland House Publishing, Inc.,
431 Harding Industrial Drive, Nashville, Tennessee 37211

Cover design by Bruce Gore, Gore Studios, Inc.
Photography by Dean Dixon Photography
Hair and Makeup by Calene Rader
Text design by Julie Pitkin

ISBN 1-58182-230-8

Printed in the United States of America
1 2 3 4 5 6 7 8 — 05 04 03 02 01

MILDRED'S MARRIED LIFE

CHAPTER I

O married love! each heart shall own,
where two congenial souls unite,
Thy golden chains inlaid with down,
Thy lamp with heaven's own splendor bright.

—LANGHORNE

WHAT A HAPPY winter that was—the first of Mildred's married life. Her cup of bliss seemed full to overflowing. She was very proud of her husband and not without reason, for his was a noble character. He was a man of sterling worth, lofty aims, cultivated mind, and polished address.

They were a pair of lovers who grew more and more enamored of each other day by day as the weeks and months rolled on.

And while the new love flooded Mildred's pathway with light, the old loves, so dear, so long tried and true, had not to be given up. She was still a member of the home circle, a sister in all its interests and pleasures, its cares and its joys.

There was no interruption of the mutual sympathy and helpfulness of mother and daughter, brothers and sisters, nor was the father deprived of the prized society of his firstborn in the family gatherings about the table or in the cozy sitting room or parlor when evening brought rest from the toils and cares of the day. She was there, as of old, ready to cheer and entertain him with music or sprightly conversation—brighter too, and more full of a sweet and gentle gaiety than of yore.

These things formed no mean or slight element in Mildred's happiness, yet there were times when it was bliss to be alone with her lover-husband in the privacy of their own apartments—the room that had always been hers and a connecting one. Both were of good size, pleasant and cheery, and made doubly attractive by the perfect neatness and various tasteful little feminine devices in which Mrs. Keith and her daughters were thought to excel.

Mildred soon discovered that her husband was far from neat and orderly in his habits. But accepting the fact as the one inevitable yet small thorn joined to her otherwise delicious rose, she bore the trial with exemplary patience, indulging in never a reproachful word or look as she quietly picked up and put in place the books, papers, and garments which he scattered here and there with reckless indifference to the consequences to them or himself.

Mildred thought her efforts were unappreciated if not entirely unnoticed until one day, on opening a drawer in search of some article which he wanted in haste, he exclaimed at the neat and orderly arrangement of its contents. "Really, Milly, my dear," he added, "I must say with Solomon, that 'he that findeth a wife findeth a good thing.' In my bachelor days, I'd have had many a vexatious hunt for things which now I always find in place, ready to my hand. It has been my daily experience since I became a benedict."

Mildred looked up in pleased surprise. "I have been half afraid my particularity about such things was a trifle annoying to you, Charlie," she said in a gratified tone.

"Not at all, but my slovenliness must have been seriously so to you," he returned, coming to her side. "I'll try to reform in that respect," he went on playfully, "and I wish that, to help me, you would impose a fine for every time you have my coat to hang up in the wardrobe, my boots or slippers to put away in the closet, or—"

"Oh, I should ruin you!" Mildred interrupted with a light, gleeful laugh.

"Not particularly complimentary that, to either my good intentions or the supposed amount of my income," he returned, bending over her to caress her hair and cheek. "Besides, it would depend largely upon the weight of the fine. How heavy shall it be?"

"Fix it yourself, since the idea is all your own."

"One dollar each time for every article left out of place, the fine to be increased to not more than five dollars in case no improvement is manifest within a month. How will that do?"

"Oh," laughed Mildred, "I shall certainly impoverish you and speedily grow rich at your expense."

"Come now, little lady, about how often have I transgressed against the rules of order in the two weeks that we have shared these rooms!"

"Perhaps twenty. I have kept no account, so can only guess at it."

"Well, really!" he sighed, in mock despair, "I could not have believed I was quite so bad as that. But that's all the more need for reform; you must insist upon the fines, Milly. I can't let you have so much trouble for nothing."

"Oh, Charlie, as if your love didn't pay me a thousand times over!" she exclaimed, looking into his eyes with dewy with mingled emotions — love, joy, and gratitude.

He answered with a tender caress and a smile of ineffable affection.

"And then you have been so generous with money, too," Mildred went on. "Why, I never was so rich before in all my life! I've not spent a fourth part of the hundred dollars I found in my purse the day after our wedding. and mother tells me you have insisted upon paying a good deal more for our board than she thinks it worth."

"Ah, dearest, circumstances alter cases. And with more knowledge, you and mother may change your minds," he replied, half absently.

Then after a moment's silence, he added, "This is my gift to my dear wife, and I cannot tell her how glad I am to be able to make it. My darling, will you accept it at your husband's hands?"

He had laid a folded paper in her lap.

"Thank you," she said playfully and with a pleased smile. "I can't imagine what it is. Why — !" she said half breathlessly as she scrutinized it with more care, then let it fall into her lap as she gazed up in to his face with an astonished, half-incredulous look. "Charlie, is it real?" she asked.

"Entirely so, dear Milly," he answered with a tender smile.

"You have endowed me with all your worldly goods," she said, half in assertion and half inquiringly.

"No, my darling, not nearly half as yet. I know you thought you were marrying a poor man—at least comparatively so—but it was a mistake. And, oh, the delight of being able to give you ease and luxury, you who have toiled so long and faithfully for yourself and others!"

He clasped her in his arms as he spoke, and with a heart too full for speech, she laid her head upon his breast and wept for joy and thankfulness that such love and tender protecting care were hers.

There was space for little else in her thoughts for the moment, and the next, she rejoiced keenly in the wealth that put in her power so much that it had long been in her heart to do for others. She rejoiced, trembling and remembering the Master's words, "How hardly shall they that have riches enter into the kingdom of God!"

If adversity had its trials, prosperity was not without its perils, and a most earnest, though silent, prayer went up that she might be kept from trusting in uncertain riches or setting her affection on earthly treasures.

"Tears, darling?" said her husband, softly stroking her hair. "I thought to give you joy only."

"They are happy tears, Charlie," she murmured, lifting her face, putting an arm about his neck, and gazing with loving eyes straight into his. "And yet—oh, I am almost afraid of so much wealth!" And she went on to tell him all that was in her heart.

"Ah," he replied, "I do not fear for you, your very sense of the danger will tend to your safe-keeping."

"Yes, if it keeps me close to the Master and ever looking unto Him for strength to resist temptation. Utter weakness in ourselves, we may yet "be strong in the Lord, and in the power of His might.'"

"Yes, you know Paul tells us the Lord said to him, 'My grace is sufficient for thee, for my strength is made perfect in weakness.'"

CHAPTER II

Wealth heaped on wealth, not truth nor safety buys;
The dangers gather as the treasures rise.

—DR. JOHNSON

DR. LANDRETH HAD an errand downtown. Mildred stood at the window looking after him with loving, admiring eyes. He turned at the gate to lift his hat and kiss his hand to her with a bow and smile, then sped on his way, she watching until his manly form had disappeared in the distance and the gathering darkness, for evening was closing in.

Even now she did not turn from the window but still stood there, gazing into vacancy, her thoughts full of the strange revelation and surprising gift he had made to her within the last hour.

She would go presently to mother and sisters with the pleasant news, but first she must have a little time alone with her best Friend, to pour out her gratitude to Him and seek strength for the new duties and responsibilities now laid upon her, the new dangers and temptations likely to beset her path.

A few moments had been passed thus when her mother's gentle rap was heard at the door of her

13

room. Mildred hastened to open it and to unfold her wondrous tale, sure of entire, loving sympathy in all the contending feelings which agitated her.

She was not disappointed. But while Mrs. Keith fully understood and appreciated Mildred's fear of the peculiar temptations of wealth, she took a more hopeful view.

"Dear daughter," she said, "trust in Him who has promised, 'As thy days so shall thy strength be,' and take with joy this good gift He has sent you. Keep close to Him and you will be safe, for 'He giveth more grace.'"

There was great and unqualified rejoicing among the younger members of the family when they learned the news—they were so glad that hard times were over for dear Milly, who had always been so helpful and kind to everybody, and so thoroughly did they believe in her goodness that they had no fear for her such as she felt for herself.

"Milly, what are you going to do with so much money?" asked Annis, hanging about her sister's chair. "You can never spend it all."

"Spend it!" cried Don contemptuously "Only silly people think money was made just to spend. Wise ones save it up for time of need."

"The truly wise don't hoard all they have, Don," remarked Ada gravely.

"No, of course they must live, and they'll pay their way honestly if they are the right sort of folks."

"And if they are that," said Mildred, with a sweet, bright smile irradiating her features, "they will feel that the money God gives them is not wholly their own to save and to spend."

"Oh no, to be sure!" exclaimed Annis. "And what a nice big tenth you'll have to give now, Milly! I wish you would find some work for me to do and pay me for it, so that I'd have more money to give to missions."

"I'll pay you ten cents for every hour you spend at the piano in faithful practice," was Mildred's answer as she playfully drew her little sister to a seat upon her knee.

"Oh, Milly! Will you really?" cried the child, clapping her hands in delight. "But that will be twenty cents a day when I practice two hours, and I mean to, every day but Sunday."

"And I make Fan the same offer," Mildred said, catching a half wistful, half eager glance from the great gray eyes of that quiet, demure little maiden.

The gray eyes sparkled and danced, their owner saying, "Oh, Milly, thank you ever so much! I'll be sure to earn twenty or thirty cents every day."

"Forty or fifty cents a day for you to pay, Milly!" Annis said in some anxiety.

"Don't be concerned, little sister. My purse can stand even so grievous a drain as that," returned Mildred merrily.

"Mildred," said Ada, sighing slightly, "I can hardly help envying you the blessing of having so much money to do good with."

"Perhaps your turn will come. At your age, I had no more prospect of it than you have now," Mildred said, gently putting Annis aside and rising to leave the room, for she heard her husband's step in the hall, and it was her wont to hasten to meet him with a welcoming smile. But pausing a moment at Ada's side, she added in an earnest undertone, "It is a great responsibility. You must help me with your prayers and sisterly warnings, to meet it aright."

A liberal gift to each benevolent enterprise of the church to which she belonged was the first use Mildred made of her newly acquired wealth. Next, her thoughts busied themselves with plans to increase the comfort and happiness of her own dear ones, after that of friends and neighbors.

There were some of these who might not be approached as objects of charity yet whose means were so small as to afford them little beyond the bare necessaries of life. Meantime, her husband was thinking of her and how he might add to her comfort and pleasure.

It was now early November, but the woods had not lost all their autumnal beauty, and the weather was unusually mild for the time of year. They had had many delightful walks and drives together.

Now Dr. Landreth proposed a trip to Chicago, and Mildred gave a joyful assent. There would be ten miles of staging, then three or fours hours of railway travel, making a journey just long enough for a pleasure trip, they thought. And a short sojourn in the city would be an agreeable variety to Mildred at least, she having been scarcely outside of Pleasant Plains for the last six or eight years.

With a heart full of quiet happiness and over-flowing with gratitude to the Giver of all good, she set about the needful preparation. No great amount of it was needed, since they were only going sightseeing and shopping. It could all be done in one day, and they would start early the next morning.

Alone in her own room, packing her trunk, her thoughts reverted to a friend, a most estimable widow lady, a member of the same church as herself, who was enduring a great fight with adversity, having an aged mother and several small children to support.

"They must be in need," Mildred said half aloud to herself, pausing in her work. "How nice it would be to give them a little help without their knowing whence it came! Yes, I shall do it."

She rose from her kneeling posture beside her trunk, went to her writing desk, enclosed a ten-dollar bill in a blank sheet of paper, and placed that in an envelope which she sealed and directed to Mrs. Mary Selby, the lady in question.

She wrote the address in a disguised hand, and following Rupert to the outer door that evening as he was starting downtown after tea, asked him to drop the note into the post office for her as he passed.

He readily complied, and her secret was between the Master and herself, as she desired it to be.

The little jaunt was an entire success, and the happy bride and groom returned from it loaded with presents for the dear ones at home. There was an easy chair for father, a handsome set of furs for mother, linen for Zillah, a silk dress for

Ada, and a fine soft merino garment for each of the younger girls. In addition, there were books and a variety of smaller gifts for all the rest, even Celestia Ann having been kindly and generously remembered.

It was a glad homecoming, a merry, happy time for all the family. And Mildred was younger, prettier, happier in appearance and manner than they had seen her for years.

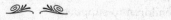

CHAPTER III

For true charity,
Though ne'er so secret, finds a just reward.

— MAY

A PART OF the winter's amusement at Mr. Keith's was the making of plans for a house to be built the next summer for Dr. and Mrs. Landreth. The doctor had bought an acre of ground adjoining Mildred's lot and intended putting on it a large, handsome residence with every modern convenience that was attainable in that region of country.

As soon as the frost was out of the ground, the work of cellar-digging and laying the foundation was begun. At that time the doctor hoped the house might be ready for occupancy the next fall, but as the weeks and months glided by, that hope grew fainter under the dilatory conduct of workmen and those who supplied material, until the most he allowed himself to anticipate was that the walls would be up and the roof on, so that work upon the inside might be carried forward during the winter.

The delay was somewhat trying to both himself and Mildred, for they had a strong desire to be in

a home of their own, though it was a very pleasant life they led in that of her parents.

Mildred kept up her church work, her Sunday
school teaching, attendance at the weekly prayer
meetings, the sewing society, etc., and also her
visits to the sick and the poor.

And now she had the happiness of being able to
provide these last with medical attendance gratis,
her husband joining her, heart and soul, in her
kindly ministrations.

The two were entirely congenial, and their love
deepened and strengthened with every day they
lived together.

One bright April day, the doctor invited his
wife to take a drive with him a few miles into the
country, on the farther side of the river, where he
was going to see a patient.

He always liked to have her company on such
expeditions, when good roads and fine weather
made the drive a pleasure, and she never let anything but sickness hinder her from going. She
never wearied of his society or begrudged the
sacrifice of her own plans and purposes to add to
his comfort or pleasure.

The intended call had been made, and they
turned their faces homeward. The sun was still
some two or three hours high, and the air was
pure and bracing, not too cool for those who were
well wrapped up. The delicate yellow green of the
newly opened buds was on the forest trees, while
at their feet the blue violet, the purple anemone,
and other lovely wildwood flowers peeped up
here and there among the blades of newly spring-

ing grass or showed their pretty heads half hidden by the carpet of last year's fallen leaves lying brown and dry upon the ground.

The doctor several times stopped his horse and alighted to gather a handful of the delicate blossoms for Mildred.

She thanked him with appreciative words and smiles, yet half absently, as though her thoughts were intent upon something else. "Charlie," she said at length, "I should like to call on Mrs. Selby. It is a little out of our way, but I think we have time, and it is strongly impressed upon me that, for some reason, we are needed there."

"Very well, dearest," he answered, stepping into the buggy again and taking the reins from her hands, "then we will drive there at once. There can be no harm in doing so, whether your impression be correct or not."

The horse was urged into a brisk canter, there were no more pauses for flower-gathering, and presently they drew up before the Selby dwelling—a plain, square log house with two rooms below and two above.

As they did so, Mrs. Selby appeared at the door, drawn there by the welcome sound of wheels.

"Oh, how glad I am to see you!" she exclaimed with tears in her eyes. "I was just asking the Lord to send me help somehow, for mother is very sick, and none of the children are old enough to go to town for a doctor. How good He is to send me just what I need!"

"Doctor and nurse both, dear Mrs. Selby," said Mildred, pressing her hand in heartfelt sympathy, for they had already alighted and the doctor was fastening his horse preparatory to entering the house.

He found the old lady very seriously ill but fortunately had the needed remedies with him.

The sun was setting when he went away, leaving Mildred, reluctantly enough, too, but there were medicines to be given at regular intervals during the night, and she was quite resolved to assist in the nursing. He could not stay, as there were other patients claiming his attention; therefore, he left her, promising to return for her at an early hour next morning.

Mildred followed him to the door.

"My darling, I can hardly bear to go without you," he said, taking her hand in his and bending his head to press a parting kiss upon her sweet lips, his eyes full of wistful tenderness. "'Tis a lonely spot," he added with an uneasy glance around upon the woods that enclosed the little clearing on every side. "No man about and not another house within half a mile; none on this side of the river within two miles."

"No, my dear husband,," she answered, looking up into his face with a sweet, trustful smile, "but you leave me in safe keeping nevertheless. 'Man is distant, but God is near.'"

"That is true," he said, "and the path of duty is the safest. You do seem to be needed here. So goodbye for a few hours, my precious little wife. 'The Lord bless thee and keep thee, and cause His face to shine upon thee.'"

"And may He keep my husband also and bring him safely back to me," she whispered, putting her arms about his neck, her lips to his.

She watched him till a turn of the road hid him from sight, then went in, and with a serene, cheerful face entered upon her gentle ministrations about the sickbed while Mrs. Selby was busied with her children and household cares.

At length, all these duties had been carefully attended to, doors and window shutters bolted and barred, and the children put to bed, where they were presently soundly sleeping.

The invalid also had fallen into a heavy slumber under the influence of medicines, and the two ladies sat down together for a little chat in the neat outer room that served as kitchen, sitting room, and parlor.

The evening was chilly, but a bright wood fire burned and crackled in the large open fireplace. They drew their chairs near to it and to each other and conversed in low tones, for the door into the inner apartment where the sleepers were stood open, and while they talked, their ears were intent to catch the slightest sound from the sickbed.

"It was so kind of you to stay with me tonight, and of the doctor to leave you," Mrs. Selby said, gratefully pressing Mildred's hand.

"I am sure you would have done the same for me in like circumstances," returned Mildred, "and who that loves the Master could do otherwise, remembering His words, 'Inasmuch as ye have done it unto one of the least of these my brethren, ye have done it unto me'?"

"I am sure He sent you and the doctor here today in answer to prayer," Mrs. Selby went on, her eyes filling with grateful tears. "I think mother would have died before morning without better help than I could give her."

"We will give Him all the praise," Mildred said with emotion. "He sent us, and I feel it very sweet to be sent on His errands." Her eyes shone as she spoke.

"Yes," was the reply, "I have found it so when He has sent me, as I am sure He sometimes has, to minister to the troubled of heart, the sick and dying. I often feel thankful, Mrs. Landreth, that money isn't always the only thing we can serve Him with, because that would shut me off almost entirely."

"No, it is not always even the best or most acceptable," Mildred said with her sweet, cheery smile.

"Yet there are times when it is more welcome than almost anything else, it being unfortunately so very necessary in this world of ours. Ah! Mrs. Landreth, even at the risk of seeming to talk a great deal about myself, I must tell you what happened to me last fall.

"I was walking into town one cold day in November, feeling so sad at heart thinking over our many necessities and how impossible it seemed to supply them. Mother needed flannel badly, and my little boys had no shoes. I was praying silently for help all the way and trying to stay myself upon God and those precious verses in the sixth chapter of Matthew about the fowls of the air and the lilies of the field, and the sweet words, 'Your heavenly Father knoweth that ye have need of all these things.' They did comfort me a good deal, but my faith wasn't strong enough to quite lift the burden off me—the need was so very pressing and there was no sign of help at hand.

"They would trust me at the stores, I knew, but to buy on credit or borrow money when you can see no way of paying it back, is, I think, no better than stealing, so I couldn't do that. And just as that thought was in my mind, I looked up and saw that I was in front of the post office. I hadn't thought of going there, because I had no reason to expect anything by mail, but I stepped in and asked if there was a letter for me.

"You can't imagine how surprised I was when they handed me one, and I tore it open and found a ten-dollar bill in it. Nothing else, not a word of writing to say where it came from. But I knew my heavenly Father had sent it, and I cried for very joy and thankfulness—behind my veil—as I walked along the street."

Mildred's heart and eyes were full as she listened. Ah, how sweet it was to have been made the blessed Master's almoner to one of His dear children! But her face was half averted lest it should betray her secret, and Mrs. Selby's own emotion assisted in the desired concealment.

"I thought I should never again doubt the love and care of my heavenly Father," the latter went

25

on after a moment's pause in which Mildred's hand sought hers and pressed it in loving sympathy. "I went to Chetwood & Mocker's and bought the flannel and the shoes. Mr. Chetwood waited on me himself, and I felt sure he put the goods down to me, probably at cost. And such a rejoicing there was when I got home! I really believe, Mrs. Landreth, that those who have but little of this world's goods enjoy them all the more, and so things are more evenly divided among us all than most people think."

The clock struck nine, and Mildred begged Mrs. Selby to lie down and try to sleep. "You know," she said with an arch smile, "the doctor's orders were that we should take turns in watching and sleeping, so that each should have half a night's rest."

"Yes, and you mean to obey, like a good little wife," returned her friend with playful look and tone. "Won't you take the first turn at sleeping?"

"No, no, I feel quite fresh, and you are looking sadly tired."

Mrs. Selby yielded and stretched herself upon a lounge, saying, "Please be sure to call me at twelve, or sooner if you feel like lying down." Then she fell asleep almost before Mildred had finished covering her carefully with a heavy blanket shawl.

Mildred sat musing by the fire for a little, then seeing it was the hour for giving medicine, administered it—the invalid just rousing sufficiently to take it and falling off into a heavy sleep again immediately—and returned to the outer room, found a book, seated herself near the light, and began to read.

She paused presently and sat for a moment noting the death-like quiet that reigned within and without the dwelling, broken only by a faint sound of breathing from the next room and the ticking of the little wooden clock on the mantel.

The fire needed replenishing. She attended to it with as little noise as possible and returned to her book.

Chapter IV

And now in moodiness,
Being full of supper and distempering draughts,
Upon malicious bravery dost thou come
To start my quiet.

—Shakespeare's *Othello*

Suddenly there came a sound as of a heavy body falling or being thrown against the outer door. Then a hand fumbled at the lock, and a man's voice said thickly, "Open hyar and let a feller in, can't ye?"

Mildred started to her feet, her heart beating fast and loud, while at the same instant Mrs. Selby, waked by the noise of the fall, raised herself to a sitting posture and glanced round at her friend with a look of alarm.

"Blast ye! Let me in hyar," repeated the voice, its owner accompanying the words with an oath and another effort to turn the handle of the door.

The two women drew nearer together.

"Who is it?" asked Mildred in a tremulous whisper.

"I don't know, but don't be frightened. He's evidently too drunk to break in on us, for the door and window shutters are stout and strongly barred."

For several minutes the man continued to fumble at the door, pushing against it and muttering curses and demands for entrance. The women stood together, clasping each other's hands and listening with bated breath.

Then he staggered to the window and tried that but with no better success.

"If ye don't le'me in," he growled at length, "I'll climb the roof and git down the chimbly."

"Could he?" asked Mildred, taking a tighter grip of her companion's hand.

"A sober man could easily get on the roof from the back shed," Mrs. Selby answered, "but I hope he will fail. He seems very drunk for such an exploit."

"But can't he reach an upstairs window from the shed roof?"

"No, there is none on that side. It's a story-and-a-half house and with upstairs windows in the gable ends only. They're without shutters, but he can't possibly reach them."

"And the chimney?"

"I don't know whether it is large enough for him to get down it or not," Mrs. Selby said with an anxious glance toward it, her ear, as well as Mildred's, still intent upon the sounds without, "or what will be the consequence if he should. There's a pretty hot fire. I hope the heat will deter him from attempting the descent, even if he should gain the roof and the chimney top."

"But if he should succeed in getting down?" Mildred said with a shudder, looking about for some weapon of defense.

"We must catch up the lamp, rush into the other room, and barricade the door. There! He is on the shed roof! Don't you hear?"

"Yes. Let us kneel down and ask our heavenly Father to protect us."

They did so, continuing their silent supplications for many minutes, all the more importunately as the sounds from overhead told them that the drunken wretch had gained the upper roof and was at the top of the chimney.

Another moment and the rattling fall of a quantity of plaster gave notice that he was actually attempting the descent.

They rose hastily, Mrs. Selby caught up the lamp burning on the table, and they withdrew on tiptoe, but with great celerity, to the shelter of the inner room.

The lamp was set down in a corner where its light would not disturb the sleepers. Then the two stood close to the door, intently listening and looking—the fire giving them light enough to see the invader should he succeed in forcing an entrance. Mrs. Selby stood with her hand upon the lock, ready to close the door instantly upon his appearance.

Mutterings and curses came faintly to their ears. These were followed by half-suppressed cries and groans and another fall of plaster, but the sounds seemed stationary; they came no nearer.

"He has stuck fast, surely!" Mrs. Selby exclaimed in an excited whisper.

"And we can do nothing to help him!" Mildred said half breathlessly.

"No, nothing."

Their conjecture soon grew to a certainty as the groans and cries continued. Gradually, their fright abated, and they stole softly back to the fireside. Pitying the sufferings of the poor wretch, they hastened to open the outer door, throw out the burning brands, and extinguish them with water. It was all they could do for his relief.

He asked for water, and they tried to give it to him but without success. He sang drunken songs, muttered indistinctly, asking, they thought, for help to get out—help they could not give. Then followed groans, cries, and ineffectual struggles to get free. These gradually grew fainter and at length were succeeded by a death-like silence and stillness.

"He is dead?" Mildred asked in an awestruck whisper.

Mrs. Selby nodded assent, tears springing to her eyes. "I am afraid so, though I had not thought it would come to that," she whispered. "Oh, how horrible it is! But I'm thankful that mother and the children have slept through it all. We"ll not speak of it to mother if she wakes. There, I hear her stirring, and it's time for the medicine again."

"I'll hold the light for you," Mildred said, taking it up and following. She could not bear to stay alone in that room at that moment.

Excitement and horror had effectually driven away from the two ladies all inclination to sleep, and the moments dragged by on leaden wings until daylight brought some small sense of relief.

As Mrs. Selby threw open the window shutters, her eyes were gladdened by the sight of a neighbor nearing her door. She hastened to admit him.

"Good morning, he said. "I'm out looking for my cow. She's strayed away, and I thought you might—But what's wrong?" he broke off abruptly, gazing at her with mingled surprise and alarm.

She pointed to the chimney and dropped, white, trembling, and speechless, into a chair.

Mildred had closed the inner door the moment his loud, hearty tones were heard at the other.

"What is it? House afire? Never mind, we'll soon have it out. Where's your water bucket?" he asked with a hasty glance about the room.

"No, no! A man—drunk—dead—I—I think" gasped Mrs. Selby.

"What! In the chimney? You don't say!" And hurrying to the fireplace, he stooped and stuck his head in. "Yes, sure enough," he gasped, withdrawing it with a shudder, "I see his legs dangling down. He's dead, you think?" he asked, turning from Mrs. Selby to Mildred.

"Yes," she said in an awed, tremulous tone. "He groaned and cried out so at first but hasn't uttered a sound for hours."

"Horrible, horrible! You don't know who he is?"

Mrs. Selby shook her head and relieved her feelings by a burst of weeping.

"And you think he was drunk?"

"I'm certain of it. The tones of his voice told it." Then, calming herself, she told the whole story in a few brief sentences. "Oh, what is to be done, Mr. Miller?" she asked in conclusion.

"I'll go for the coroner, and we'll have him got out and taken away just as soon as it can be done according to law."

"But your cow?'

"No matter about her. I'll send my boys to look her up."

He hurried out and away.

At the same moment, the sound of wheels sent Mildred to the outer door.

Giving the reins to a plainly dressed elderly woman who sat in the buggy with him, Dr. Landreth leaped to the ground, and in an instant his wife was in his arms, hiding her face on his breast and sobbing hysterically.

"What is it, my darling?" he asked. "The old lady—is she so much worse?"

Mildred seemed unable to speak, and Mrs. Selby answered for her. "No, doctor, I think mother is better, but—" and the story of the night's alarm was repeated.

"Dreadful! What a night you two must have passed!" commented Dr. Landreth, holding his wife closer to his heart.

"Who on airth can it be?" exclaimed the woman in the buggy, who had listened to the recital in open-mouthed astonishment, as she spoke leaning down and forward in an effort to look in at the open door, till she seemed in imminent danger of falling.

"I haven't an idea," returned Mrs. Selby. "But excuse me, won't you alight and come in, Mrs. Lightcap? I ought to have asked you before but hadn't noticed that you were there."

"Yes, thank ye, I'll 'light. I want to peek up in that chimbly. And besides, I've come to stay all day and as much longer as you need help or nursin'. You've nursed my folks and me in many a sick spell, Mrs. Selby, and I'm glad o' the chance to pay ye back in your own coin," the woman answered, jumping out and hitching the horse as she spoke.

"It's very kind—" Mrs. Selby was beginning, but the other interrupted her. "No, 'tain't nothing o' the sort! I'd a ben an ungrateful wretch if I hadn't a clapped on my bonnet and come the minute the doctor told me you was wantin' help."

They hurried in in the wake of Dr. Landreth and Mildred.

Stooping his tall form on the hearth, the doctor put his head into the chimney, took a long look, then withdrawing it, said in low, moved tones, "Yes, he is there, and life seems to be extinct. There is not the slightest sound or movement."

"And ye can't so much as give a guess who he is? Just let me look," said Lightcap, thrusting him aside in her eagerness.

The doctor stepped toward Mrs. Selby and, speaking in an undertone, said, "Keep this from your mother if possible. I will see the coroner and tell him how important it is that she should not be disturbed by noise or excitement."

"Then we must keep it from the children," she returned, with an involuntary glance at Mrs. Lightcap.

"Yes," said the latter, "we'll manage that. Let's get 'em up, give 'em their breakfast, and send 'em off somewheres out o' the way afore the crowner comes."

"Can I see my patient now? I must get my wife home as soon as possible," the doctor said with an anxious glance at Mildred's pale cheeks and heavy eyes.

"She'd ought to have a bite o' breakfast first," Mrs. Lightcap remarked. "What's in that basket in the buggy, doctor? Shall I fetch it in?"

"Ah, I forgot!" he exclaimed. "I'll go for it. Mother sent it, with a message to you, Mrs. Selby, that she did so because she knew you would be too busy to do much cooking just now."

"Just like her—always so thoughtful and kind," Mrs. Selby said gratefully. "I'll have mother ready to see you in a few moments, doctor, but Mrs. Landreth must have a cup of tea before she takes her ride. I've a fire kindled in the stove in the shed kitchen and—"

"And I'll get the breakfast while you tend to your mother and the children," interrupted Mrs. Lightcap, bustling about like one perfectly at home and in earnest to accomplish a great deal in the shortest possible space of time.

Half an hour later, Mildred was driving home by her husband's side, drinking in deep draughts of the fresh morning air, scented with the breath of wildwood flowers, and rejoicing that every step was taking her farther from the scene of last night's horror and affright.

At the bridge they met the coroner and his jury on their way to hold the inquest over the dead man.

"Good morning, doctor. Good morning, Mrs.

Landreth. Do you come from Mrs. Selby's?" asked the coroner, pausing and lifting his hat to Mildred.

Dr. Landreth reined in his horse to reply.

"Yes, Mr. Squires, and I hope you will manage the affair as quietly as possible, as the old lady is quite ill, and excitement would be very injurious to her."

"Certainly, we'll do our best, doctor. The man will have to be got out of the chimney, and we'll hold the inquest nearby in the woods. But you and your wife will be wanted as witnesses."

"Sure enough!" exclaimed Dr. Landreth. "I had not thought of that. And, really, my wife ought to go home and to bed at once." And he turned to her with an anxious, questioning look.

"Yes, let us go back, Charlie," she said in an undertone, though her heart sank at the very thought. "I can stand it if I have you with me."

"And it may be well for me to be there in case the old lady grows worse," he said, turning the buggy round as he spoke. "Can you spare me while I drive the children over to the nearest neighbor's, Milly?"

"Oh, yes, for it will be a great relief to poor Mrs. Selby to have them out of the way," she answered, thinking of everyone before herself, as was her wont.

Driving so rapidly as to arrive some time before the coroner and his men, who were on foot, the doctor explained all to Mrs. Selby, taking her aside, out of hearing of the children, then quickly gathered them into his buggy and drove off by another road before the other party came in sight.

The men had brought ladders for climbing and implements suitable for breaking a hole in the chimney large enough for the corpse to be drawn through. They worked from the outside and with as little noise as possible. Doors were kept closed, and the old lady, still under the influence of the medicines, slept quietly till all was over.

Mrs. Selby, Mrs. Lightcap, and Mildred were summoned in turn to tell all they knew about the case.

Mrs. Lightcap did not feel at all nervous or frightened, but the other two were much agitated and could hardly have passed through the ordeal without the support of Dr. Landreth's presence and sympathy.

A crowd had gathered, and some among them were able to identify the dead man as a confirmed, worthless sot from a neighboring town, one of the many thousand wretched victims of King Alcohol.

At last all was over, a verdict rendered in accordance with the facts, the corpse removed, the crowd scattered, and poor, weary Mildred carried home by her anxious husband to a mother and sisters scarcely less solicitous on her account.

CHAPTER V

A babe in the house is a wellspring of pleasure.

—TUPPER

SPRING AND SUMMER had waxed and waned, and the gorgeous October hues were again upon tree and shrub, their soft mellow haze everywhere, on prairie, forest, town, and river.

Annis was not ill-pleased to be sent on an errand that gave her a long walk in the sweet, bracing morning air.

She came hurrying home in almost breathless excitement, rushed upstairs, and entered Mildred's half-open door.

"Oh, Milly! What do you think? I—"

But Mildred held up a warning finger.

"Excuse me, I forgot," and Annis's voice sank to a whisper. "I didn't wake him, though," she said, stealing on tiptoe to the side of the cradle and bending down over the tiny sleeper. "Oh, Milly, but he is a beauty! Even prettier than Zillah's boy. Don't you think so?"

"Don't ask me, and don't tell Zillah what you think about it," returned Mildred with a half-amused smile. "But what did you—Ah, I see you have a letter for me," she said, holding out her hand for it.

"Yes, from Cousin Horace," Annis answered, putting it into Mildred's hand. "And see! I have one from Elsie. And, oh, Milly, they want us to come there to spend the winter, Elsie says. Do you think—"

"Us?"

"Yes, Brother Charlie, you, and me—Fan too, if she will go, but I 'most know she won't."

"I doubt if you or I will, either. I wouldn't leave Charlie, he wouldn't leave his patients, and baby is too young, I fear, for so long a journey."

Annis's countenance fell. "Oh, Milly! And I do so want to go! You don't care much about it, I suppose, because you've been there once, but I never have."

"Well, dear, we'll discuss the question when your brother comes in," Mildred said, her eyes remaining upon the open letter in her hand. "Yes, this is from Cousin Horace, and I see it contains a very warm invitation from himself, his wife, and Elsie to all four of us—Charlie, my two little sisters, and myself."

"Well, I'll go away till Percy wakes," Annis whispered. She gave another admiring look at the sleeping babe and then stole on tiptoe from the room.

She found her mother, Ada, and Fan in the sitting room, all three busy with the fall sewing for the family.

Her story was told in a breath. "See, mother, see? A letter from Elsie!" she cried, holding it up while her face glowed with animation and delight. "And, oh, Fan, she wants us to go and spend the winter at the Oaks. And Milly had one from Cousin Horace too, and—"

"One what?" interrupted Ada, smiling amusedly into the bright, eager face.

"Letter, to be sure. Oh, mother, do you think we can go?"

"You two, all alone? No indeed, my child."

"I'll not go!" exclaimed Fan with decision. "I wouldn't leave mother and father and home so long for anything in the world!"

"No, not alone, mother. Brother Charlie and Milly are invited. But I'm not sure, after all, that I do want to go and leave you," Annis sighed, taking a stool at her mother's feet and laying her head in her lap.

"And what could mother do without her baby?" Mrs. Keith said, smoothing the bright curls with a softly caressing hand. "But we will not try to decide it all in a moment, dear. I doubt if the others go, and if they do not, of course, that will settle the question for you."

"There's Brother Charlie now!" Annis exclaimed. "Yes, I hear his step on the stairs. Milly will show him the letter now, and I hope he'll say he can go. Mildred says she wouldn't go without him."

Mildred looked up with a smile as her husband entered, stepping softly that he might not disturb the slumbers of his little son and heir.

He bent over the cradle for an instant, then drew near and sat down by her side.

"How would you like to go south for the winter?" he asked.

"Accept the invitation to the Oaks, do you mean?"

"I had not heard of it," he said in some surprise, "but as matters are, I think it will be the very thing to do."

He went on to explain that business of importance called him to the neighborhood of his old home and was likely to keep him there for several months. "And of course," he concluded, "I want to take my wife and boy with me. Will you go, love?"

"Must you go? I don't think I could stand so long a separation," she said, a slight mist coming over her sight at the very thought. "But isn't our boy too young for such a journey?"

"No, I think not. He is a strong, healthy little fellow, and the journey, if we start within a week, need not subject him to much exposure or fatigue. Can you get ready in that time? I find it is quite important for me to go."

"Yes, I can if necessary."

"This is Wednesday," he said. "Suppose we consider it settled that we are to start next Tuesday morning."

"Very well. Fan and Annis are included in the invitation from the Oaks. Are you willing to take charge of them in addition to wife and child?" she asked with playful look and smile.

"Certainly," he answered, "the more the merrier."

The babe woke, Mildred took him up, presently gave him to his father, and they went downstairs to let Annis know their decision and to "talk the matter over with mother and the rest."

As they entered the sitting room, Annis looked up with an eager "Oh, Brother Charlie, will you go?" while Fan dropped her work and, holding out her arms for the babe, asked if she might not take it.

"Not just yet, Aunt Fan," the doctor said with a good-humored smile, dandling the babe as he spoke. "Papa must have him for a little while."

"Till he begins to fret or cry," remarked Ada laughingly. Then you'll be very ready to resign him to the first one who offers to take him."

"Of course, isn't that the way fathers always do?" the doctor answered with imperturbable good nature. "Yes, little sister," he said to Annis, "we are going. Expect to leave here for the sunny South on the morning stage next Tuesday. Are you going with us?"

"Going where? South, did you say?" asked a merry voice from the open doorway.

All turned toward the speaker. It was Zillah standing there, making a beautiful picture with her babe in her arms, a sweet, fair, chubby little fellow, pink-cheeked, dark-eyed, and older by a month or more than Mildred's boy.

Down went Fan's work again, and with a bound she was Zillah's side, holding out her hands to the child with a "Come to your auntie, sweet, pretty pet!"

Zillah graciously resigned him, and accepting the chair gallantly offered by the doctor, she asked again what their talk was about.

"Suppose I read Cousin Horace's letter aloud," said Mildred, taking it from her pocket.

"And Elsie's, too," said Annis, laying it in her lap.

With Mr. Keith and Rupert coming in at that moment, followed almost immediately by Wallace and Donald, she had the whole family for an audience. Annis silently took possession of her father's knee, and as Mildred finished, with her arm about his neck whispered in his ear a coaxing entreaty to be allowed to accept Elsie's invitation.

"Wait a little, pet, till I hear what Brother Charlie has to say. But how are father and mother to do without you for so long a time?" he said, holding her close with repeated caresses.

"Maybe you'll enjoy me all the more when I come back," was the arch rejoinder.

"Ah, child, as if you were not already the very light of our eyes! But there, we must stop talking and hear what the doctor is saying."

The matter was under discussion for some time. Fan remained steadfast to her resolution to stay at home; Annis urgently wished to be permitted to go. Before night, she had won the consent of both parents, letters of acceptance had been dispatched to the Dinsmores, and active preparations for the journey were set in motion.

The child's heart misgave her now and then at thought of the long separation from home, parents, and so many of her dear ones. But the time was so short for all that had to be done to put her wardrobe in such order as mother and sisters deemed desirable that she was kept in a whirl of excitement that up to the last hour had left her little leisure for dwelling upon anything but the business in hand and the pleasure in store for her at the journey's end.

The parting was a hard one when it came. She went away drowned in tears and sobbing pitifully but presently forgot her grief in the interest of new scenes and soothed by the kindly ministrations of her brother and sister.

CHAPTER VI

Slow pass our days in childhood—
Every day seems like a century.

—BRYANT

AT THE OAKS, Elsie waited for Annis's answer to her letter with an eager impatience which she found it difficult to restrain. Her papa was closely questioned in regard to the exact length of time it must necessarily take for the one missive to travel to Indiana and the other to wend its way to the Oaks. Then she counted the days, settled upon the earliest possible as the one on which to expect it, and from then on watched the mails and was sorely disappointed each time one arrived without bringing what she so greatly desired, for the letters from Pleasant Plains were delayed, as will occasionally happen.

On the third morning, her father, glancing over the letters he had just taken from the mailbag, remarked, "None yet from Mildred."

"Oh, dear!" she sighed, "won't you write again today, papa? Don't you think our letters must have been lost on the way?"

"We will wait a little longer, daughter," he said with a sympathizing look and smile. "Letters will travel slowly sometimes. You must try to be patient, and perhaps this afternoon's mail will bring the news we are so desirous for."

"I wish you would let me write to Annis again this morning, papa, instead of learning lessons," she pleaded.

"No, my child, I wish you to attend to your studies as usual," he replied with gentle decision.

She said no more, for she was never allowed to question his decisions or to urge the request he had once denied.

At the regular hour, she repaired to her pretty boudoir, took out her books, and set to work at her tasks but not with her usual spirit and energy. Her thoughts kept wandering to Annis and Mildred, and she found herself repeating words and sentences without in the least taking in their meaning.

She delighted in most of her studies, but Latin, which she had begun only of late, she thoroughly detested. Still, her father required her to study it, and she was too docile and obedient to think of refusing, which indeed would have been quite useless, as he was one who would be obeyed.

But having spent a half-hour or more over the morning's allotted portion, and finding she knew no more about it now than on opening the book, she grew discouraged and sought him in his private room, where he was busy at his writing desk.

"Well, daughter?" he said inquiringly as he perceived her standing, book in hand, close at his side.

"Oh, papa, this is such a dreadfully long, hard lesson! I can't learn it!"

"Can't! Ah, that's a lazy word!" he said pleasantly, laying down his pen to put his hand caressingly on her drooping head. "Surely my brave little girl is not going to allow herself to be conquered by difficulties!"

"Papa, you don't know how difficult it is for a little child like me," she sighed. "Why must I learn Latin?"

"Because your father bids you," he answered in a grave, slightly reproving tone. "Is not that a sufficient reason for a good, obedient child?"

"Yes, sir, but—"

"Well?"

"I was just going to say the lazy word again, papa," she said, furtively brushing away a tear.

He pushed back his chair and drew her to his knee. "What is wrong with you today?" he asked, smoothing the hair back from her temples with a gentle, caressing hand.

"I don't know, papa. It seems as if I can't study somehow."

"Do you know your other lessons?"

"Yes, sir. I learned them yesterday."

"Go and get your books, and I will hear them now and here."

She obeyed and recited almost perfectly.

He gave the deserved meed of praise, then taking up the Latin grammar said, "This lesson must be learned, but I shall not require that today. I am in an indulgent mood," he went on with a fond, fatherly smile, "and you shall have a holiday. Your mamma and I are going to drive into the city, and will take you along, if you wish to go."

"Oh, papa, how nice!" she cried, clapping her hands. Then, throwing her arms round his neck to hug and kiss him, she said, "How good of you! Thank you ever so much! I shall try hard to learn that lesson tomorrow."

"And will succeed, I haven't a doubt," he said, returning her caresses. "Now run away to Aunt Chloe, and tell her I want you handsomely dressed—in the dark blue velvet suit—and at once, for the carriage will be at the door directly."

"Yes, sir!" And away she flew, her face sparkling with delight.

"Why, darlin', you looks mighty pleased," remarked Aunt Chloe as the little girl appeared before her fairly dancing in the exuberance of her joy.

"Oh, yes, mammy, so I am, for I'm going to drive to the city with papa and mamma instead of sitting here studying that hard lesson. So, you must please make all the haste you can to dress me in my blue velvet suit."

"Massa say so? Den 'dat I will, darlin', hab you ready befo' Miss Rose gits her bonnet on."

Always ready to exert herself for the pleasure of her idolized nursling, Aunt Chloe had laid aside her knitting and taken the dress from the wardrobe before her sentence was fairly concluded.

Her dexterous fingers made quick work of the little girl's preparations. "Ki, chile, but you is lubly and sweet as de rose!" was her delighted exclamation as she took a careful survey of her completed work.

"Oh, mammy, you mustn't flatter me!" laughed

Elsie, dancing from the room. "Goodbye till I come back."

Hastening to the grand entrance hall of the mansion, she found the carriage at the door, but her papa and mamma had not yet made their appearance. Her baby brother was there, however, crowing in his nurse's arms.

"Oh, you pretty darling. Come to sister!" cried the little girl, holding out her arms to receive him.

But her father's step and voice sounded in her rear. "No, no Elsie! He is quite too heavy for you to hold, especially with his outdoor garments on."

"Why, papa, you never said so before," she returned in a disappointed tone, looking up entreatingly into his face as he drew near, "though you've often seen me holding him."

"But he is growing heavier every day, daughter, and for your own sake I must forbid you to carry him. You may have him on your lap occasionally for a little while at a time, when you are seated, but never hold him when standing."

Elsie sighed, then brightening said, "I was ready quickly, papa."

"Yes, dearest, and I am altogether satisfied with your appearance."

"As you well may be, my dear," added Rose merrily, joining them at that moment.

Mr. Dinsmore handed her into the carriage, then Elsie, followed them himself, and taking the babe from his "mammy," bade her get in also.

"I shall hold Master Horace for a while," he said, "but if he begins to fret or cry, I shall hand him over to you."

The day was a glorious one in late October. The carriage was roomy, softly cushioned, and easy rolling; Dick was a skilful driver; the roads were in fine condition;, and the little party were in high health and spirits. Elsie quite forgot her disappointment of the morning and was full of innocent mirth and gladness.

Arriving in the city, they spent some hours in shopping, visiting in turn dry goods, jewelry, book, and toy stores, and Elsie became the delighted possessor of several new books and a lovely doll to add to her already large family. All were gifts from the fond, indulgent father, who seemed ready to give her everything that money could buy for which she showed the slightest desire.

Nor was he less indulgent to his wife, but fortunately, neither wife nor daughter was disposed to tax his generosity to any great extent.

They drove to the post office last and to Elsie's great delight found there a letter addressed to her papa from Mrs. Landreth, enclosing a few lines from Annis to herself, both accepting the invitation to the Oaks and mentioning the day set for the beginning of their journey. Mildred also told what route they would take and about how soon they expected to reach their destination if all went well by the way.

"These letters have been delayed," Mr. Dinsmore said when he had read his aloud to Rose and Elsie,. "and if our friends are not detained, we should have them with us day after tomorrow."

"Oh, oh, how nice!" cried Elsie. "Papa, must I say lessons the first day they're with us?"

"There will not be another holiday for you until that troublesome Latin lesson has been properly disposed of," he answered gravely.

"If it isn't ready for you tomorrow, papa, it shan't be for want of trying," Elsie said resolutely, though it cost an effort to refrain from again complaining that it was too long and hard for her to master.

But she felt rewarded by the affectionate, approving smile her father bestowed upon her. And she said to herself, "What a very naughty, ungrateful girl I should be not to try my very best when papa has been so good and kind to me today! Yes, and is every day. I don't believe any other little girl ever had such a dear, good father."

And with the thought, she lifted her face to his with such a sweet, loving look, as she sat opposite him in the carriage, that he could not refrain from taking her in his arms and bestowing upon her another and another tender caress.

Rose watched them with a beaming countenance. It was a perpetual feast to her to behold their mutual affection.

As they drew near home, they were overtaken by a gentleman on horseback. Mr. Dinsmore saluted him with great cordiality.

"Ah, Travilla, how are you? All well at Ion?"

"Quite well, thank you, Dinsmore," returned the cavalier, lifting his hat and making a low bow first to Mrs. Dinsmore and then to Elsie. "Just coming from the city?"

"Yes, and glad we are reaching home in time to receive your call."

"Thank you. I was so fortunate as to meet with entire success in the business you entrusted to me, Dinsmore, of which fact I think we shall presently have ocular demonstration."

"And in that case there will be other demonstrations," responded Mr. Dinsmore, looking at his little girl with an odd sort of smile.

"I dare say," Mr. Travilla said, smiling admiringly at her also.

They had turned in at the great gates and now swept rapidly and smoothly along the broad graveled drive that, winding about through the well-kept grounds, finally brought them to the principal entrance to the mansion.

The carriage stopped, and the door was thrown open by a servant who stood there in waiting. Mr. Dinsmore sprang out and assisted his wife to alight, then Elsie.

As the little girl's foot touched the ground, she caught sight of a beautiful little phaeton to which were harnessed a pair of Shetland ponies, very pretty and exactly alike.

"Oh!" she exclaimed. "We must have company! I wonder who it is with such a lovely turnout?"

"No, Miss Elsie, dar ain't no comp'ny in de house," put in the servant, her papa's man John, "and I kin' o' reckon dat grand turnout b'longs hyah. Ain't dat so, Massa Horace? Yah, yah!"

Elsie gave her father an eager, inquiring, half-incredulous look.

"Yes, daughter, it is yours," he said, smiling fondly upon her.

"Oh, papa, how good you are to me!" she cried, glad, grateful tears shining in her eyes. "Is this lovely turnout really my very own? And may I get in and take a drive?"

"Yes," he said, leading her to the phaeton, handing her in, then seating himself by her side and taking the reins, which John put into his hand.

"The phaeton is just large enough for two," he remarked, "and the ponies, though small, are quite strong enough to draw us both. You shall have the reins in your own hands presently, and I will give you a lesson in driving, though you already have a pretty correct idea of it."

"Why, yes, papa, you know you have let me drive a little several times. And these pretty ponies are so small I think I can easily manage them. Will you let me drive by myself sometimes?"

"You would prefer my room to my company, eh?" he remarked laughingly.

"Oh, I didn't mean that, papa!" she cried, blushing vividly.

"I intend to let you drive about the grounds with Annis, or some other friend, when you have become familiar with your new steeds," he answered, bending down to touch his lips to the glowing cheek. "And I hope, my darling, you will find great enjoyment in so doing."

A few weeks previous to this, Elsie had seen and admired a similar though less handsome equipage, and though she did not ask for such a one for herself, her ever-indulgent father had at once determined in his own mind that she should have it.

He wanted it to be a pleasant surprise, so he

said not a word to her about it but talked the matter over with Rose and his friend Mr. Travilla. The latter undertook to make the purchase for him and had managed the business to the entire satisfaction of all concerned.

"Papa, you are too good to me!" Elsie cried.

"Am I?" he asked, putting the reins into her hands. "Now let me see how well you can drive?"

She succeeded very nicely in guiding and controlling her small steeds, so well indeed that her father said she might try it alone in a day or two. They made the circuit of the grounds, then drew up in fine style before the veranda, where Rose and Mr. Travilla sat watching them.

"Well and bravely done, my little friend!" exclaimed the latter, springing down the steps to hand her from the phaeton as John took the reins, she resigning them a trifle reluctantly.

"Oh, it's so nice!" she cried. "Please, papa, mayn't I drive round once more?"

"No, this is enough for today. Let Mr. Travilla lift you out. You must remember you have already had a long drive, besides the fatigue of shopping."

Mr. Dinsmore spoke kindly but with decision, and the little girl submitted without so much as a pout or frown. She spent a moment or two petting and caressing the new ponies, her father and Mr. Travilla looking on and listening with pleasure and amusement, and she ran happily into the house, eager to show her friend the books and toys just brought from the city.

He was a frequent visitor at the Oaks, made

much of Elsie, and always showed as keen an interest in her childish pleasures as Mr. Dinsmore himself.

"Isn't she a beauty, Mr. Travilla?" Elsie asked, exhibiting the doll.

"That she is. She will be your favorite child, I presume."

"No, sir. She will be valued very highly as papa's gift, but she can never be so dear as Rose."

"Rose? Which is she?"

"My very largest dollie, the first that papa ever gave me. She's been with me through so many happy times, and sad times, that I love her better than I can ever love another."

"Ah!" he said with sudden gravity, for her words carried him back to a time that had been very sad indeed to her and to all who loved her.

"Mr. Travilla, may I name this one Violet, for your mother?" she asked.

"Certainly, my dear. My mother will feel complimented no doubt," he said with a twinkle of fun in his eye. "You must have quite a family, I suppose. Would you like to show them all to me?"

"Oh, indeed, sir, if you care to see them! There are more than a dozen, big and little, altogether."

"It is about time you were having your hat and coat taken off, daughter," her father said, coming up to them at that moment.

"Yes, papa, I'm going now, and Mr. Travilla is going with me to see my baby-house and all of my family."

"Ah, won't you invite me too?"

"Why, papa!" she exclaimed, "You don't need

an invitation. You have more right in my rooms than even I have."

"By virtue of being the grandfather of the family, I suppose," he said laughingly. "Well, then, I will lead the way."

The baby-house was really very handsome, and the dolls, all tastefully dressed, presented a pretty sight.

"I'm afraid I'm growing rather old to play with dolls," remarked Elsie with gravity when she had given their names and relationship. "But I like to make pretty clothes for them, and that teaches me to cut and fit and sew. And when I'm reading here by myself, I like to have Rose on my lap. She seems like a live thing and is company for me."

"You find that pleasanter than studying Latin?" her father said in a playful tone, laying a hand lightly on her head and bending down to look fondly into the sweet child face.

"Papa, I do mean to have that lesson perfect tomorrow," she said in a half-whisper, her eyes cast down and her cheek flushing.

CHAPTER VII

Oh, enviable, early days!

—BURNS

MR. TRAVILLA LEFT the Oaks directly after tea. Mrs. Dinsmore went to the nursery, and Elsie and her papa were the only remaining occupants of the parlor. He was pacing to and fro in a meditative mood; she was seated by the center table, turning over her new books.

Presently pushing them aside, she asked, "Papa, shall I get my Latin grammar and learn that lesson now?"

"No, you are tired and will find it easier in the morning. Besides, I want to talk to you now. Come here," he said, taking possession of an easy chair beside the bright wood fire that crackled on the hearth.

She obeyed with joyous alacrity.

"You are pleased with the phaeton and ponies?" he said inquiringly as he drew her to his knee.

"Yes indeed, papa! What does make you so very, very good to me?"

"Love," he answered, holding her close. "My darling, there is nothing I enjoy more than giving you pleasure and adding to your happiness. Tell me if you have a single wish ungratified."

"Only one that I can think of just now, papa," she replied, looking up at him with an arch smile, then dropping her eyes and blushing as if more than half ashamed of the admission.

"And what is that?" he asked.

"I don't like to tell you, papa," she murmured, hanging her head still lower while the blush deepened on her cheek.

"Ah, but you have roused my curiosity, and now I insist upon knowing," he said, with a mixture of authority and playfulness.

His left arm encircled her waist, and he put his right hand under her chin, lifting her face so that it was fully exposed to his view.

"Now look up at me and tell me what you wish. Why should you desire to hide a thought from the father who loves you as his own soul?"

"Only because I'm—I'm ashamed, papa. It's just that I—I wish you wouldn't make me learn Latin."

With the last word she turned and hid her blushing face on his breast.

He did not speak for a minute or more.

"Please don't be vexed with me, papa," Elsie said with tears in her voice.

"No, daughter," he answered gravely, "but I see that if I would consult my child's best interests I must content myself to leave some of her wishes ungratified. You are not old enough or wise enough to choose for yourself in such matters. And I am sorry that you are not quite willing to submit to my guidance and authority."

"Don't be sorry, papa! I will be good about it after this, indeed I will!" she said with earnest entreaty, looking up into his face with eyes full of tears. "I'm glad I have a papa who loves me well enough to always do what he knows is best for me, even when I am so naughty as to—to not want to do as he says."

Rose came in at that moment, and Mr. Dinsmore's only answer to his little girl was a silent caress.

She came to him the next morning before breakfast, her face beaming with satisfaction, her Latin grammar in her hand.

"Good morning, papa," she said. "I know every word of my lesson now. I rose half an hour earlier than usual and studied hard all that time and while mammy was dressing me and curling my hair."

"That is like my own dear little girl," he responded with a pleased look, taking her on his knee to kiss her. He kept her there while he heard the lesson.

"Very well done, indeed!" he said when she had finished. "Now you see what you are capable of when you resolutely set your mind to your task. Your phaeton is at the door. Would you like to take a drive about the grounds before breakfast?"

"Yes indeed, dear papa! I shall enjoy it ever so much now that that hard, disagreeable lesson is out of the way."

"We shall have a full half-hour for it," he remarked, consulting his watch. "Run to Aunt Chloe and have yourself well wrapped up, for the air is keen and frosty."

He did not need to bid twice, nor did she keep him waiting. She was at his side again in hood and cloak by the time he had donned his overcoat and gloves.

He rode with her but let her do all the driving. He brought her back in good time for breakfast, and she came to the table happy as a lark, eyes shining, and with a lovely color in her cheeks.

"Oh, mamma," she said, "we have had such a nice drive in the new phaeton, papa and I, and he says I may drive Annis about the grounds when—"

"If Annis is willing to trust herself to your driving," put in her father laughingly.

Elsie's countenance fell slightly. "I hope she will be. The ponies seem very gentle and tractable," she went on. "You know you said so yourself, papa."

"Yes, I don't think there will be any danger, or I should be very sure not to risk my child in the venture," he returned, smiling with fatherly affection into the fair young face.

"No doubt about that," said Rose. "But, Elsie, are Annis and your papa to be the only persons to enjoy the privilege of driving out with you in the new phaeton?"

"Oh, mamma, would you be willing to try it?" Elsie asked with eager delight. "I'll drive you out today when my lessons are done, if papa gives permission and you will go. May I, papa?"

"You may do anything your mamma wishes you to do."

"Unless," said Rose, "I should unwittingly ask her to do something her father has forbidden."

"Oh, of course! That might happen, but in any conflict of authority, undoubtedly mine must stand against all other, since even you have promised to submit to it, lady mine," Mr. Dinsmore returned in a jesting tone and with a fond, lover-like look into the sweet face of his wife.

Elsie glanced wonderingly from one to the other.

"Did you really, mamma?"

"Yes. Didn't you hear me?" said Rose, laughing and blushing.

"But don't you do exactly as you please?"

"I have so far."

"That's because she's wise and good enough always to please to do right," remarked Mr. Dinsmore.

"Oh, yes, sir!"

For the next five minutes Elsie ate in silence, apparently lost in thought.

Her father watched her with an amused face.

"Well, daughter," he said at length, "a penny for your thoughts."

"I was only thinking, papa, that I hope I'll never have to get married," she said with a slight sigh.

"Of course you will never be compelled to," he replied, with difficulty restraining a laugh, "but what is your objection?"

"I mean if I should have to promise to obey. Because I couldn't obey two people, if they didn't always agree, and I shall always have to obey you."

"Well, my child, you need not so much as have a thought about that question for ten years to come," he answered with gravity. "It is a subject a little girl like you should never think of at all."

"Then I'll try not to any more, papa. But, mamma, you haven't said whether you will drive out with me today or not."

"Thank you for your kind offer," Rose answered. "But I think I must wait until another day, as there are some things I wish to attend to in preparation for the coming of the cousins tomorrow."

"Can you not allow yourself a little playtime?" her husband asked. "Your company will not arrive until near tea-time tomorrow evening."

"Well, perhaps. You will send the carriage to meet them, of course?"

"Yes, and ride over myself on horseback."

"Oh, could I drive over for Annis?" asked Elsie.

"No, it would be too long a drive for you. But if you wish, you may ride with me—ride Glossy or Gyp, either one would be the better for the exercise."

"Thank you, dear papa. I believe I shall like that quite as well," the little girl responded with a very pleased look and smile, for there was scarcely anything she enjoyed more than riding by her father's side.

She was quite fearless and at home on horseback, having been accustomed to it ever since she was five years old.

Rose was very busy that day and the next in preparations for the comfort and enjoyment of her expected guests.

Elsie took a deep interest in all that was done and gave such assistance as she was capable of and permitted to attempt. She was with her mamma in the suite of rooms intended for the use of Dr. and Mrs. Landreth, watching and helping her as she put the last finishing touches to their adornment: placing vases of flowers on mantels and dressing and center tables, looping anew the rich curtains of silk and lace, rearranging their soft folds and then stepping back to note the effect, pushing an easy chair a little further to this side or that, picking up a shred from the carpet, or wiping invisible dust from some article of furniture.

"Your Cousin Mildred is extremely neat, Elsie, is she not?" Rose asked, taking a final survey of the beautiful boudoir.

"I believe she is, mamma, but not more so than you are," the little girl answered, looking up affectionately into the slightly anxious face of her young stepmother.

"You think she will be pleased with these rooms?"

"Oh, mamma, how could she help it? They are just lovely! They are sweet with the breath of flowers, and everything corresponds so nicely. You know papa chose all the furniture, carpets, curtains, and ornaments, and he has such excellent taste."

"So you and I think, at all events," Rose responded with a smile.

"And Cousin Mildred is lovely enough to match with everything here," Elsie remarked, sending a satisfied glance from side to side.

"Are you not glad she is coming to make us a good long visit, mamma?"

"Yes, dear, I am indeed, for though I have never met her, I feel quite sure, from all your father, Mrs. Travilla, and you have told me, that I shall love her dearly."

"I think she will be like a sister to you, and Annis like one to me, and that we shall have oh such a nice time while they stay!"

"Yes, I hope so. But haven't we nice times always with each other, your dear father, and Baby Horace?"

"Yes, yes indeed, mamma! I often think I must be the happiest girl in the world," Elsie said, putting her arm about Rose's waist and holding up her face for a kiss.

Rose gave it with earnest affection. "Dear child," she said, "I hope, if the will of God be so, life may always be as bright to you as it is now. Darling, I think even your fond father can hardly love you much better than I do. Ah," she added, taking out her watch, "it is time you were getting ready for the ride with him to the depot."

At that, Elsie hastened from the room. As she descended the broad staircase, her father appeared at its foot, looked up smilingly at her, and held out his arms.

With a merry, ringing laugh she sprang into them and put hers about his neck.

"My darling!" he said, holding her close. "I was just coming for you. I have ordered the horses, and they will be at the door by the time you can don your riding habit."

CHAPTER VIII

Youth treads on flowers where'er he goes,
And finds on every thorn a rose.

"WE ARE ALMOST there! Time to don hats, gloves, and cloaks and gather together bags, boxes, and bundles," exclaimed Dr. Landreth in his cheery tones, retrieving Annis's hat from the rack overhead as he spoke. "Milly, my dear," he added, bending over her in tender solicitude, "how is the headache now? I'm thankful I shall soon have you out of this close, overheated atmosphere. No, don't disturb yourself, Annis and I will take care of the bundles. Now give me the boy."

"Here," he called, beckoning to the porter as the train came to a standstill, "carry out these packages, will you? Now, Milly and Annis, keep close to me, but don't be uneasy. This is the end of the road, and we have plenty of time."

Annis had hurried to put on her wrap, and now, catching up her satchel, turned to her sister, who was fastening her cloak, and said, "Oh, Milly, make haste, and I'll keep close behind you."

"No, go on, child," Mildred answered, gently pushing the little girl on before her.

Another minute and they were assisted from the car by their Uncle Dinsmore on one side and Cousin Horace on the other. There was Elsie, too, waiting to give a welcoming embrace to each, and beside her stood Mr. Travilla, who had ridden over to meet his old friend, Charlie Landreth, and be introduced to his wife, for the mistress of Ion had so often sounded Mildred's praises in her son's ears that he was very desirous to meet the object of her encomiums.

Tired and travel-stained as she was, Mildred did not show to the best advantage, yet the beauty of form and feature, the intellectual and sweet countenance, seemed to him to fully justify his mother's praises.

With joyous exclamations of "Oh, Elsie, dear!" "Oh, Annis, how glad I am you've come at last!" the little girls clasped each other in a warm embrace.

Greetings, introductions, and friendly inquiries exchanged all around, the travellers were speedily bestowed in Mr. Horace Dinsmore's comfortable family carriage and driven away in the direction of the Oaks, their luggage following in a wagon.

Elsie was lifted to her saddle by her father's strong arms; he vaulted to the back of his own larger steed; and with the older Mr. Dinsmore and Mr. Travilla having mounted theirs, all four started at a gallop in pursuit of the carriage, which they presently outdistanced, exchanging smiling salutations with its occupants as they passed.

Elsie rode by her father's side, the other two gentlemen a little in advance.

"You will go on to the Oaks with us, father? And you, Travilla?" Mr. Horace Dinsmore said with hospitable cordiality.

"Not tonight, Horace," the old gentleman answered. "I'll be over tomorrow, if nothing happens to prevent. I want a talk with Mildred, but she's tired tonight and ought to retire early."

Mr. Travilla also declined the invitation, on the plea of an engagement to meet a man on business.

So, presently, when they reached the spot where their roads parted, Elsie and her papa were left to pursue their way alone.

"Now for a race to the Oaks, Elsie," Mr. Dinsmore said merrily. "Let us see if we can get there in time to receive our friends on their arrival."

So the horses were urged till they almost flew over the ground. Elsie had never ridden so fast before, and she enjoyed it keenly.

They arrived so much in advance of the carriage that she had time to run to her dressing room and have her riding habit exchanged for a white cashmere and pink ribbons, then join her papa and mamma in the principal entrance hall as the carriage drew up before the door.

The warmest of welcomes awaited the weary travellers. "Never were guests more welcome!" was Mr. Dinsmore's salutation.

Rose embraced Mildred with sisterly affection, saying, "I am so very glad you have come. I am sure we shall love each other."

"I do not doubt it," Mildred answered. "I was prepared to love you for your husband's sake, and now I see that I shall for your own."

"And, mamma, this is Annis," Elsie said, releasing the latter from a vigorous hug and drawing her toward Rose. "Annis, this is my pretty new mamma that I told you I was going to have, when I was at your house."

"She is pretty and looks very kind, too," Annis exclaimed, in a burst of honest admiration.

"Thank you, dear," said Rose in evident amusement, bestowing a loving kiss upon the child.

Mr. and Mrs. Dinsmore themselves conducted their older guests to the apartments prepared for them, Annis and Elsie following.

"Oh, how charming!" was Mildred's delighted exclamation when shown into the beautiful boudoir, from which open doors gave glimpses of dressing and bedrooms equally inviting in appearance. Turning with beaming countenance to her hospitable entertainers, she said, "What a haven of rest after our long, weary journey!"

"I hope it may prove so indeed," Rose said, looking greatly pleased.

"We want you to make yourself perfectly at home in our house, Milly," added Mr. Dinsmore. "You, too, Charlie. Call for anything you want; a servant will always be ready to answer your ring. And do not feel that you are trammelled by any of the rules of our establishment. Rise in the morning and retire at night, come and go, as you like. We will be glad of your company when you are disposed to favor us with it, but when you prefer the solitude of these rooms, do not hesitate to indulge that preference," he concluded laughingly as he withdrew, presently followed by his wife.

Meanwhile, Elsie, after allowing Annis a hasty survey of Mildred's apartments, had taken her into an adjoining bedroom, saying, "Now, Annis, dear, you are to choose between this room and another next to my sleeping room. Mamma said so because she was not sure whether you would care most to be near Cousin Milly or near me."

For several minutes, Annis gazed about in silence, seemingly struck dumb with surprise and admiration by the richness and beauty of her surroundings.

A velvet carpet covered the floor, lace curtains draped the windows, the bedspread and pillow shams were of pink silk covered with a film of lace, chairs and couches were cushioned with satin damask, and sweet-scented hothouse flowers and a variety of other pretty things were scattered here and there with a lavish hand.

"Oh," she cried at last, drawing a long breath, "what a lovely room! It's fit for a queen, I am sure! Did Cousin Rose really intend it for me?"

"Yes, if you prefer it to the other, Annis. But won't you see that before you decide? I should so like to have you close beside me," Elsie said, half imploringly, putting an arm about Annis's waist and drawing her toward a door opposite that by which they had entered the room.

"And I'd like it, too," Annis returned with hearty acquiescence. "And in fact," she went on, "I'd rather not be where everything is so handsome and costly, because I might spoil something."

"That wouldn't make any difference. 'Tis easy to replace things, and one grows tired of always seeing the same," Elsie said. "But I think the other room is quite as pretty in every way as that."

She had led Annis into a back hall, and they were now descending a flight of stairs that led to another on the ground floor. Reaching that, they presently came to a door which, on opening, admitted them to a bedroom that was, as Elsie remarked, quite equal to the one they had just left.

"This is it, Annis," she said. "That door yonder opens into my sleeping room, and you can get to Cousin Mildred from here very quickly and easily by the way we came."

"Oh, I'll take this!" said Annis. "'Twill be ever so nice for us to be close together!"

"Oh, won't it! I'm so glad. Come and see my rooms if you're not too tired." Elsie led the way, Annis following, through bedroom, dressing room, and boudoir.

They were so large and airy—and so luxuriously and beautifully furnished and adorned—that Annis almost thought herself in fairyland.

She said so to her little cousin, adding, "What a happy girl you must be! You seem to have nothing left to wish for."

"'A man's life consisteth not in the abundance of the things which he possesseth,'" Elsie murmured half aloud, half to herself. Then, turning to Annis a very bright, winsome face, she added, "You know, Jesus said that when here on earth, and though I am very happy, I sometimes think I could be just as happy in a hut with His love and my dear papa's."

"Yes," assented Annis, "I wouldn't be without

father and mother for all the money and fine things in the world. But oh, isn't it time for me to be getting washed and dressed?"

"Yes. I'll have your trunk carried to your room," Elsie said, ringing for a servant. "And mammy will help you dress, if you wish. Oh, here she is!"she said as the old nurse appeared before them. "Mammy, this is Cousin Annis Keith. You remember her, don't you?"

"Yes, 'deed I do, darlin'," she returned. "I'se glad to see you at de Oaks, Miss Annis, and hopes you and my chile hab best ob good times togedder," she added, dropping a curtsy to the young guest.

"Thank you, Aunt Chloe," Annis said, shaking hands with her.

"Yes, mammy, we're going to be close together. So please have Annis's trunk brought immediately to that room," Elsie said, indicating with a motion of her hand the adjoining apartment, for they were now in her own sleeping room.

"Bress yo' heart, honey. I'll see 'bout dat 'dreckly," and Aunt Chloe hurried away in search of the luggage and a man servant to carry it in.

"Is Cousin Horace near you at night?" asked Annis.

"Yes indeed!" Elsie replied with a joyous look and tone. "That door beside my bed leads into the room where he and mamma sleep. Their bed is very near it too, and papa always sets the door wide open before he gets into bed, so that if I want him in the night, I have only to call out 'papa,' and he is beside me in an instant. Oh, it's so nice, Annis! I feel so glad and safe with my dear earthly father so close to me, and our heavenly Father always with us, taking care of us all. You know, the Bible says, 'Behold he that keepeth Israel shall neither slumber nor sleep.' Aren't they sweet words?"

Mr. Dinsmore sat alone in the library reading by the light of the astral lamp on the center table. A door on the farther side of the room opened softly, a little white-robed figure lingered for a moment on the threshold, then with noiseless steps stole swiftly to the back of his chair. Two round, white arms crept about his neck, a soft cheek was laid against his, and a low sweet voice murmured in his hear, "My papa! My own, own dear papa!"

The book was hastily closed and thrust aside, he turned half round in his chair, caught the little graceful figure, and drew it to his knee to caress it with many an endearing word.

"Where is Annis?" he asked at length.

"Taking a bath while mammy unpacks her trunk. Then mammy will brush her hair for her and help her dress."

"Ah! I hope she will find herself quite refreshed and with a good appetite for her supper. Are you not fatigued after your long ride?"

"A little, papa."

"Then sit here and rest for the present; and you and Annis would do well to retire early to your beds tonight. I should advise her to defer even an introduction to the dolls and their house until tomorrow."

"I can hardly help wishing tomorrow was here," exclaimed the little girl. "I'm in such a hurry to show her Gyp and Glossy and the two new ponies and the phaeton."

"And ever so many other things? Well, my child, go to bed early, and tomorrow will soon be here. I shall give you a holiday for the rest of the week, so that you and Annis may get your fill of play and find lessons enjoyable by next Monday."

"Oh, how nice, papa!" she cried, giving him a hug.

"But I thought you were fond of lessons," he said, pinching her cheek and smiling fondly down into the bright little face.

"Yes, papa, so I am usually, but I like a holiday now and then. And may I drive Annis out in the phaeton every day?"

"You may, when there is nothing to prevent— two or three times a day if you wish. But you will want to ride sometimes. The Shetlands can be used in the saddle, and I think it will be the best for Annis to learn on, if, as I suspect, she has never ridden."

"And you will teach her, papa? No one could do it better."

"If she wishes. But Dr. Landreth and Mr. Travilla are quite as capable, and she may prefer to learn from them."

"I don't believe she will. I'm sure I'd much rather have you than anybody else."

At that, he only smiled and stroked her hair.

CHAPTER IX

A sweet, heart-lifting cheerfulness,
Like spring-time of the year,
Seemed ever on her steps to wait.

—MRS. HALE

"WILL I DO, Elsie?" asked Annis.

"Yes indeed! What a pretty dress. It is so soft and fine and just matches your blue eyes."

"Dat's so, chile, sho' nuff," said Aunt Chloe, smoothing down the folds of the pretty cashmere, "an' de ribbons de same. Now, missy, I'se done, an' dar's de suppah bell."

Annis thought again that it was like being in fairyland, as Elsie, putting an arm about her waist, drew her on through several spacious, richly furnished, softly lighted rooms to one more brilliantly illuminated, where a table was spread with the choicest china and silverware and all the delicacies of the season.

Mr. and Mrs. Dinsmore were already there, and as the little girls came in at one door, Dr. and Mrs. Landreth entered by another.

Mildred had exchanged her travelling suit for a becoming evening dress and seemed to have shed much of the weary look she had worn on arriving.

The doctor, too, was greatly improved in appearance by a change of linen and riddance of the dust of travel.

When all had been seated, the blessing asked, and the meal fairly begun, Annis, smiling across the table at her sister, asked, "What have you done with Percy?"

"Found a nurse for him and left him in her care fast asleep," replied Mildred. Then turning to her Cousin Horace, she remarked, "Good help is still scarce with us. A competent child's nurse is not to be had, but with so many sisters at home, all esteeming it a privilege to assist in the care of the baby, I scarcely felt the need of one there."

"You must have one here, though," he answered with good humor, "for we are not going to let you shut yourself up at home to such cares and labors while there is so much enjoyment to be had in riding, driving, and visiting among this hospitable and cultivated people."

"I agree with you entirely in that, Dinsmore," chimed in the doctor. "I brought her here to recruit and enjoy herself as much as possible."

"Indeed!" Mildred said with an arch look and smile. "I understood it was because you couldn't do without me and your boy."

"For both reasons, my dear, and so loath am I to be parted from you that I shall find very little pleasure in visiting old friends, and old familiar haunts, unless I can take my wife along."

"I hope you gentlemen will allow us some quiet home pleasures also for a variety," remarked Rose. "I have been planning the enjoyment of some interesting books and many a chat with Cousin Mildred."

"Discussing the affairs of the nation?" asked Mr. Dinsmore with a twinkle of fun in his eye.

"Perhaps they may be the theme occasionally," she answered demurely, "when we have exhausted those, to us, more important topics — husbands, housekeeping, and babies."

"For those shall you require secret sessions, deliberating behind closed doors?" asked the doctor.

"Perhaps. That you will learn in due time. Cousin Mildred, I have learned that, like myself, you have a great fondness for both books and music."

"Yes, and I have been rejoicing in the certainty that plenty of books worth reading will always be found where Cousin Horace is."

From that, the talk turned upon books and authors.

The little girls, both sufficiently intelligent and well informed to understand and appreciate the remarks of the elders, were quiet but interested listeners. Mr. and Mrs. Dinsmore were attentive to their wants as well as to those of the older guests, and the table was well served by several skilled waiters.

There was an hour of pleasant conversation in the parlor, after leaving the supper room, then the travellers bade good night to their host and hostess, pleading fatigue as an excuse for retiring so early.

"Don't stay in your cousin's room talking, but let her get to bed and to sleep at once," Mr.

Dinsmore said to Elsie as the little girls were about to leave the room.

"Yes, papa," Elsie answered. Then, going to his side and speaking in an undertone, she asked, "Mayn't I come back to you for a little while? You know it is not my bedtime yet."

"Yes, if you choose."

"You know, papa, I always do like to sit here a little while just the last thing before going to my room for the night," she said a few minutes later as she took possession of his knee.

"Not better than I like to have you do so," he answered, putting his arm about her. "Whatever should I do without my little daughter?"

Rose, sitting on the opposite side of the fire with her babe in her arms, regarded them with loving, admiring eyes.

"What are the plans for tomorrow's enjoyment with Annis, little girl?" she asked with real motherly interest.

"I think we'll drive about a good deal, mamma. Papa says we may, just as much as we please."

"Always supposing you will remember to have mercy on the ponies," he added playfully.

"Oh, yes, sir! Yes indeed! Please say how long you think that we may drive without hurting them at all?"

"I presume a couple of hours of moderate exercise will not injure them," he answered, still using his playful tone.

"I suppose we shall have callers from Roselands and Ion tomorrow," Rose remarked to her husband.

"Yes, no doubt. And I think we should give a family dinner party as soon as our friends have had time to recover from the fatigue of their journey."

"Our Ion friends to be included, of course?" Rose said, half inquiringly, half in assertion.

"Oh, yes. I have few relatives who seem nearer than Travilla and his good mother. She was, as I believe I have told you before, an intimate and dear friend of my own mother. What is it, Elsie?"

The little girl was sitting in silence on his knee, her eyes fixed thoughtfully upon the carpet, and a slightly troubled look had come over her face.

"Please don't ask me, papa," she said, blushing.

"But I have asked you."

"I — I was only thinking if Enna comes with the rest — "

"Well," he said as she paused, seemingly unwilling to finish her sentence.

"Oh, papa, I oughtn't to think unkind things! I'll try not to."

"I'm not going to have you abused," he said, after a moment's silence. "So, if Enna gives you any trouble with the ponies, or in any other way, I'm to know it. Remember that." Then, kissing her two or three times, he added, "Now say good night to your mamma and go to your bed."

Elsie lingered for a moment, clinging about his neck and gazing into his eyes with a wistful, half-pleading look.

"No," he said, in answer to her mute request. "I shall not have Enna domineering over you in her accustomed fashion, and if she attempts it, you are to tell me all about it. Will you obey me in this?"

"Yes, papa. I know I must," she said with a slight sigh and a look of some surprise that he should ask the question. "Good night."

As she left the room, he turned to his wife with the remark, "Enna is the most insufferably arrogant girl, and there would be no limit to her ill treatment of Elsie if I did not insist on being informed of it. And it is hard for her either way, poor child, for she has no fancy for telling tales."

"That is why you so seldom invite Enna here or take Elsie to Roselands?"

"Precisely."

Rain was falling heavily when Elsie woke the next morning. She started up in bed and sat for a moment listening to it with a feeling of keen disappointment, for evidently there could be no outdoor amusement while the storm lasted. "But our kind heavenly Father sends it, and he knows and always does what is best for us," was the quickly following thought. "Besides, there are ever so many pleasant ways of passing the time in the house. I wonder if Annis is awake?"

Slipping out of bed, she ran lightly across the room and, peeping in at the open door, saw that her cousin was still sleeping soundly.

At that moment, her father's voice was heard from the opposite doorway. "Elsie, my child, don't run about in your bare feet," he said. "The morning is damp and chilly, and you will take cold."

She turned at the first word, ran to him, and before the sentence was finished, he had her in his arms.

Lifting her up, he laid her in her bed again and drew the covers closely about her, saying, "Lie still now until you are warm." Then, bending down to caress her, he said, "Here are your warm slippers and dressing gown close at hand. Why did you not put them on, as I did mine?"

"I didn't stop to think, papa," she answered, putting an arm round his neck. "Good morning, you dear father, you're as careful of me as if I were a wax doll."

"A great deal more so," he said with playful look and tone. "It would be an easy thing to replace a wax doll, but money wouldn't buy another little girl like mine. How it storms outside!" he exclaimed, glancing toward the windows. "I am sorry for your sake, but you and Annis shall have every indoor enjoyment I can give you."

"Yes, papa, thank you. And I know we'll have a nice time. Just think of all the lovely dolls and toys you have given me and that will be new to Annis. And I've so many nice books and pictures, and there's the piano and—"

"Well, that will do for the present. I'm glad I have a little girl who can bear disappointments cheerfully. Lie still until the fires here and in your dressing room are well under way and the rooms comfortably warm," he said, as he left her, closing the door after him.

"Elsie, are you awake?" asked Annis from her room.

"Yes, but papa won't let me get up yet. Oh, don't you want to come and lie here beside me till

I may? If you won't catch cold coming. Please put on your slippers and dressing gown first."

"Catch cold just running across two rooms with such soft warm carpets on the floor?" laughed Annis, hastening to accept the invitation. "I'm not so delicate as all that, Miss Dinsmore. Oh, isn't it good to be here with you, you darling!" she said, creeping close to Elsie and hugging her tight. "Except when I think of mother and father so far away" she added with a sigh, the tears starting to her eyes for an instant.

"Yes, I'm so sorry for that!" Elsie returned with warm sympathy. "How nice it will be when we all get to heaven and never have to part anymore!"

There was a moment's thoughtful silence, then a talk beginning with regrets that the storm would prevent their intended outdoor diversion was soon exchanged for plans for passing their time delightfully in the house.

Annis had naturally a great flow of animal spirits, and there had been nothing in her life thus far to check it. Sheltered in the home nest, the youngest of the tribe—and as such shielded, adored, and indulged by parents, brothers, and sisters—she had known nothing of care, sorrow, or labor beyond what her young strength could easily endure. Merry, frank, fearless, affectionate, and thoroughly conscientious and true, she was the most suitable and enjoyable of companions for Elsie.

The two appeared at the breakfast table with very bright, happy faces. Indeed, the weather did not seem to have a depressing effect upon anyone's spirits. The talk about the hospitable board was merry and lively, the travellers reporting themselves greatly refreshed and strengthened by a good night's sleep and ready to enjoy books, work, or play.

"What has Elsie proposed for your entertainment today, Annis?" asked Mr. Dinsmore.

"Oh, we're going to have a fine time with the dolls and baby-house the first thing. I've had a peep at them already and never did see such beauties!" exclaimed the little girl in a burst of admiration.

"Ah,' said her interlocutor, smiling. "And there will be a tea party or two, I suppose? Well, when you tire of the dolls, we'll find something else."

"Are they prettier than Mildred's and my dollie, Annis? asked the doctor.

"Oh no, Brother Charlie, of course not! And I forgot, we did think we'd have a little play with the live babies first of all. I haven't seen little Horace yet at all."

"Nor I Cousin Milly's baby," put in Elsie, "because he was so sound asleep when you came."

"We'll have them both brought to the parlor after prayers, shall we not, cousin?" Rose said, looking at Mildred, who gave a ready assent to the proposal.

"By all means," laughed the doctor, Let us introduce them to each other and satisfy ourselves by comparison which is the finer child. No doubt we shall all agree."

"Agree to disagree, probably," said Mr. Dinsmore. "I am entirely satisfied that no finer child than ours can be discovered anywhere. And I know Rose and Elsie are of the same opinion."

"Yes," remarked the doctor, "I see it in Elsie's eyes. But no matter, I have Mildred and Annis to side with me in the same opinion of our bairnie."

"Ah, don't be too sure of Annis! She may prove more unprejudiced than you suppose," laughed Mr. Dinsmore.

The others laughed in turn as Annis quietly remarked, "Percy is quite as pretty and smart as any baby could possibly be, Cousin Horace."

And it was evident that her opinion remained the same even after she had looked with delight and admiration upon the undisputedly bright and beautiful babe Mr. Dinsmore so proudly claimed as his own.

"Ours is the largest," Elsie said when the two were brought into the parlor. "But, oh, cousin, yours too is so sweet and pretty! Papa, he can't be quite so heavy as Horace. May I take him?"

"If his mother is willing, you may hold him on your lap while you sit still in that low chair. I don't forbid you to hold Horace in that way, but you are not to carry either of them about."

"Your father is wise and kind in making that rule, Elsie," said the doctor. "Little girls like you very often suffer serious injury from carrying younger children. I wouldn't advise you to do much of it, Annis."

"Oh, I'm so strong it can't hurt me, Brother Charlie," answered Annis merrily, but Mildred said, "I'll see that she doesn't do much of it."

When the babes were carried away to the

nursery, the little girls deemed it time to busy themselves with the dolls.

But first, Mildred and the doctor were taken in to see Elsie's rooms and the baby-house, Mr. and Mrs. Dinsmore going along.

"Oh, what a lovely boudoir!" Mildred exclaimed, making a critical and delighted survey of it. "Elsie, dear, it is fit for a princess! And full of evidence of a fond father's taste and affection," she added, with a glance at her cousin, whose hand was toying with his daughter's curls as she stood at his side.

Elsie's eyes were lifted to his face with a loving, grateful look as she answered, "Yes, Cousin Milly, and that's the very best of it."

Annis grew enthusiastic over the dolls, saying, "So many and so beautiful! Why, some of them are very like real live babies!" she cried. And when Elsie opened a deep drawer in a bureau and displayed quantities of pretty dress materials ready to be made into garments for them, besides ribbons, laces, and flowers, all intended for their adornment—although each had already several changes of raiment—her eyes fairly danced with delight.

The morning was all too short for the fascinating employment of turning over all those lovely things and exercising taste and skill in making them up into dresses, bonnets, etc.

Elsie said her father had been on the point of buying her a sewing machine but had decided that she must first become an accomplished needlewoman.

A little while before dinner, Mr. Dinsmore came in and made them leave their sewing for a romping play because, he said, the exercise would do them good.

The evening was spent very pleasantly in the parlor with the older people, who joined with them in some quiet games. When separating for the night, all agreed that, in spite of the inclemency of the weather, the day had been a short and enjoyable one.

CHAPTER X

Oh, happy you! who, blest with present bliss,
See not with fatal prescience future tears,
Nor the dear moment of enjoyment miss
Through gloomy discontent or sullen fears.

MORNING BROKE BRIGHT and clear. The little girls took a short drive before breakfast and a longer one soon after, the attractions of the ponies and phaeton quite eclipsing for the time those of dolls and baby-house.

Annis was taken to the stables to see Elsie's other two ponies—very pretty creatures of larger size than the Shetlands—and a number of fine riding and carriage horses belonging to Mr. and Mrs. Dinsmore. She was pleased with the sight and eager to learn to ride.

"I never was on horseback," she said, "or ponyback either," she added laughingly. "But I've always wanted to learn, more than ever since I saw you on your pony the other day, Elsie. It seemed so easy and so nice for you to ride him."

Mr. Dinsmore, who was with them, offered to teach her and to give the first lesson that afternoon.

"Thank you, Cousin Horace, I'll be very glad to have you do so," he said. "But you'll be pretty sure to find me very awkward and will have many a laugh at my expense, I daresay."

"I hope we shall not show ourselves so rude as that," returned Mr. Dinsmore pleasantly, "or be so unreasonable as to expect good horsemanship from you at the start. Elsie had been riding for several years when I first took her in hand, yet I found there were some things relating to the art that I could teach her."

"And papa is such a nice teacher, Annis," Elsie said, looking up at him with loving admiration. "He never calls you stupid and never gets the least bit out of patience, no matter how dull or awkward you are."

"Elsie makes a good trumpeter without any instruction in that line," was Mr. Dinsmore's laughing comment on her remark.

The little girls had driven to the stables, and the pretty phaeton stood before the door with the ponies still attached.

"Papa," said Elsie, "I have taken Annis all round the grounds twice. May we go outside now?"

"Yes, if you will accept my escort, but not otherwise."

"Oh, we'll be only too glad, papa!" was Elsie's eager rejoinder. Turning to a servant, Mr. Dinsmore bade him saddle a horse for him to ride.

They drove several miles, Mr. Dinsmore keeping by the side of the phaeton all the way and making himself extremely pleasant and entertaining.

When they came in sight of the house, again a carriage stood before the front entrance.

"Ah! I thought we should have callers from Roselands today," remarked Mr. Dinsmore.

"And from Ion too, papa," said Elsie as a second carriage came into view.

"Yes, I see. Mrs. Travilla must be here, for her son never comes in that when alone."

The Ion carriage had arrived first. It was more than an hour now since Mildred had been summoned to the drawing room to meet the elderly lady she had learned to love so dearly in her former visit to this region of country.

They met in a close, tender embrace, followed by a long talk seated side by side and hand in hand on a sofa, while Rose entertained Mr. Travilla on the farther side of the spacious apartment.

Dr. Landreth came in from a walk and was greeted as an old friend, and the babies were brought from the nursery to be duly admired and caressed.

These last were still engrossing the attention of their elders when Mr. and Mrs. Dinsmore from Roselands and Miss Adelaide were announced.

Mrs. Dinsmore, as richly and merrily dressed as of yore, but looking still more faded and worn, especially in contrast to the fresh young beauty of her daughter, greeted Mildred with languid affection, nodded to the other occupants of the room, and sank into the depths of an easy chair as if completely exhausted by the unusual exertion.

Mr. Dinsmore's greeting was warm and hearty. "Glad, very glad to see you, Milly, my dear. Young and fresh still—and why shouldn't you be?—but growing more like your mother.

And that's the highest compliment I could pay you or anyone."

"Yes," sneered the lady in the easy chair, "Mr. Dinsmore has an eye for the charms of every woman except his wife."

But no one heeded or seemed to hear the remark.

Mildred had taken the hand of the younger lady, saying, as she gazed with affectionate admiration into the blooming face, "And this is Adelaide? You were but a child when I saw you last—eight years ago."

"And now I am very nearly as old as my Sister Rose, who is already a wife and mother," was the smiling rejoinder.

"Rose must have married very young," said Mildred, looking admiringly at her cousin's wife.

"My mother thought so," said Rose playfully, "and for Adelaide's sake, I shall now deny it."

At this moment, her husband came in with the two little girls. Fresh greetings had to be exchanged and Annis introduced to those present who had never seen her before.

Elsie glanced about the room and felt a sense of relief in perceiving that Enna was not there.

Mildred noticed that while Mr. and Mrs. Travilla and Adelaide all greeted the little girl with affectionate warmth, her grandfather and his wife returned her respectful salutation, the one with cool indifference, the other with scarcely concealed aversion.

Her father saw it, too. His cheek flushed, his eye flashed, and beckoning Elsie to his side, he put his arm about her and held her there, now and then caressing her hair and cheek with his other hand while he conversed with his friends.

"Horace," his stepmother remarked in a tone of impatience, when at length a pause in the conversation afforded an opportunity, "it is perfectly absurd—the way you have of hugging and caressing that great girl as if she were nothing but a baby!"

"Well, madam," he returned with a slight smile, "so long as it pleases her and myself, I cannot see that anyone else need object. When you are tired of it, Elsie," he added, gazing fondly down into the sweet little face now blushing rosy red and half hidden on his shoulder, "I shall stop."

"I'm not tired! I never shall be tired of it, papa!" she answered with impulsive warmth. "But," and her voice fell almost to a whisper, "mayn't Annis and I run away now for a little while?"

"Yes," he said, releasing her, and with a sign to Annis, who rose and followed with joyful alacrity, she hastened from the room.

The two were presently busy again with the dolls and their adornments, chatting and laughing happily together as they worked.

"Annis, don't you think I have just the nicest, kindest father in the world?" asked Elsie.

"Except mine; he is just fine as good and kind to me."

"Oh, yes, of course! I forgot Uncle Stuart."

"I don't—" began Annis, then checked herself and began anew. "Does Cousin Horace never call Aunt Dinsmore mother?"

"No," Elsie said with a look that seemed to say such an idea had never before occurred to her. "She isn't his mother."

"Just as much as Cousin Rose is yours," returned Annis.

"But mamma is so sweet and kind, and—"

"And Aunt Dinsmore isn't?" laughed Annis. "I don't think I'd want to call her mother myself or grandmother, either."

"I don't believe she will ever let anybody call her grandma," said Elsie.

"Cousin Adelaide's nice, isn't she?"

"Yes indeed! She was so, so kind and good to me once when I was very sick and papa was away! I love her best of all my aunts, Lora next."

Just then, there was a tap at the door and Adelaide came in. "Well, little ones," she said in a lively tone. "I have run away from the older people to see what mischief you two are at. Making doll clothes, eh? If I had my thimble here I'd help. As it is, I must try to be content to look on and perhaps favor you with a valuable suggestion now and then," she went on, taking satisfied possession of an easy chair. "We are all going to stay for dinner, by urgent request of our host and hostess."

"Oh, Aunt Adie, I'm so glad!" exclaimed Elsie, "for I want you to see my new ponies and phaeton."

"Yes, Rose told me about them. I shall expect an invitation to drive with you someday. Annis, your younger cousins—Louise, Lora, Walter, and Enna—are expecting the pleasure of calling upon you this afternoon. Lessons prevented this morning. By the way, Elsie, what has become of yours?"

"Papa has given me a holiday for the rest of this week."

"How he indulges you!"

"Yes, auntie. But am I not kept to lessons more steadily than Enna is?"

"Yes, a good deal more. I don't think he spoils you with all his indulgences."

A bell rang, and Elsie, putting down her work, said, "It's time to dress for dinner, Annis. Aunt Adie will excuse us."

"I'll go with you," Adelaide said, following them into the dressing room. "I want to see what you have that is new and pretty, Elsie. Your papa is always buying you something."

"Yes, and tell me what to wear, auntie. Papa often does, but he didn't today."

Adelaide, going to a wardrobe, took down one beautiful dress after another and finally selected a pale blue of some sort of silk and wool material, very soft and fine, delicately embroidered and edged with rich lace in neck and sleeves.

"There, that must be very becoming, I know, though I have never seen you in it," she said.

"Dat's so, Miss Adelaide, my chile look mighty sweet in dat dress," remarked Aunt Chloe, taking it from her hand and hastening to array her nursling in it. Adelaide opened a bureau drawer and then a jewel case, taking from the former a handsome sash that matched the dress in color and from the latter a pearl necklace and bracelets. "These will go nicely with it," she said.

"Oh, how lovely!" cried Annis, hurrying in from her room. "Cousin Adie, will you fasten my dress, please? I can do everything else for myself but not that very well."

"Yes, dear. Excuse my neglect in not offering you help with your preparations," Adelaide answered. "How pretty and becoming this peach-blossom dress is! But, like Elsie, you have a complexion which everything suits."

"Hers is much prettier than mine, though," was the modest rejoinder.

Adelaide thought, as she glanced from one to the other, that it would be difficult to find anywhere two more attractive-looking children.

The impromptu dinner party seemed quite a grand affair to little home-bred Annis. Yet, seated between Elsie and Mr. Travilla, who was a general favorite with little girls, she felt but slight embarrassment and really enjoyed herself very much.

She and Elsie returned with the older people to the drawing room and were chatting together beside a front window when a carriage drove up and two very stylishly dressed young ladies alighted, followed by a little girl and boy.

"Are they the cousins from Roselands?" Annis asked.

"Yes," Elsie said. "Oh, I hope they won't want to take you away from me! I heard grandpa say to Cousin Milly that of course you must all spend part of your time at Roselands."

"I don't want to," whispered Annis as the drawing room door was thrown open and the new arrivals were announced.

The greetings and introductions over, Lora seated herself near her younger cousin and niece and opened a conversation, questioning Annis about her journey and the family at home and expressing the hope of soon seeing her at Roselands.

Then Walter and Enna came up, looking eager and excited, and asking both together to be shown the new phaeton and ponies.

"How did you know of them?" asked Elsie.

"How shouldn't we know when the servants are going back and forth all the time?" returned Walter. "I say, Elsie, have them harnessed up now and let me drive them. Won't you?"

"Ask papa about it, Walter, he is the one to decide."

"No, you ask him. He'll maybe say no to me, but he won't to you."

"I don't know," Elsie returned with a slight smile, "he has often said it to me when he didn't approve of my wishes. But I'll ask him." And she went at once to him with the request, where he sat on the other side of the room talking with Mrs. Travilla and Cousin Mildred.

"Walter has learned how to drive and I think may be trusted if he promises to be gentle with the ponies and not use a whip," Mr. Dinsmore answered. "But they are yours, daughter, and you yourself shall decide whether you will lend them to him or not."

"Thank you, papa," she said, and went slowly back.

"Well, what did he say?" asked Walter.

"That I might decide it myself. Walter, will you promise to be kind and gentle and not touch my ponies with the whip?"

"Pshaw! What a question! But I promise. How long can I have them?"

"For half an hour, and to drive only about the grounds," said Mr. Dinsmore, coming up to the little group. "I don't want them tired, for I have promised to give a certain young lady a riding lesson with one of them this afternoon."

"Half an hour! That's no time at all!" pouted Enna.

"What difference does it make to you!" asked Mr. Dinsmore.

"Why, I'm to go with him, of course!"

"Wouldn't it be more polite to let Annis go? Annis, you needn't be afraid to trust to Walter's driving."

"Oh, no, Cousin Horace! But as I have been twice already in the phaeton, I should prefer to have Enna go this time," Annis answered with hearty entreaty.

"They are at the door now. I ordered them some time ago, knowing that some of you would like to take a drive," Mr. Dinsmore said.

Walter and Enna hurried from the room without waiting—the one to urge Annis to go, or the other to thank her for giving up in her favor.

When they came back, they did not look as if they had enjoyed themselves greatly. Enna was pouting, and Walter's face was flushed and angry.

"I'll not take her again," he said aside to Elsie. "She did nothing but abuse me all the way because I wouldn't let her drive, and three or four times she tried to jerk the reins out of my hands."

"Oh," exclaimed Elsie, "I'm so glad it was not I who was driving!"

"Why?"

"Because I should have had to tell papa all about it."

"You don't tell tales!" exclaimed Walter with a look of surprise.

"I dislike to very much indeed!" she answered, her cheeks growing hot, "but papa has ordered me to tell him whenever Enna tries to domineer over me, and you know I have to obey him."

"Yes, that is quite true. Horace is one of the sort that won't let you off any way at all. It's hard on you, too. But I'll tell you what, I'll warn Miss Enna, and maybe it'll make her behave herself when she's with you."

CHAPTER XI

I shall the effect of this good lesson keep.

—SHAKESPEARE

"SISTER MILLY, MAY I come in?"

It was Annis at the door of Mildred's boudoir, where she sat meditating with her babe in her arms.

"Yes, dear, I'm glad you came," she answered in low, sweet tones. "I don't see much of you now that Elsie has taken possession," she went on, smoothing her little sister's hair with tender hand as the child knelt at her side to caress little Percy.

"'Tisn't because I don't love you just as well as ever!" Annis answered with quick, impulsive warmth, holding up her face for a kiss, which was given very heartily. "I wouldn't be here without you, Milly, for anything. And yet I'm have the very nicest kind of a time. Sometimes I think its just like a fairy tale with so many lovely things about, and Elsie dressed liked a princess, and the ponies and phaeton, the beautiful dolls and all."

Mildred laughed a little and stroked the soft curls again.

"And you are enjoying yourself, dear?"

"Oh, yes, yes indeed! But—" she said, sighing

and laying her head against Mildred's knee, "I wish I could see father and mother! It makes me the least little bit homesick once in a while to see Cousin Horace with Elsie."

"Yes, my little sister, and I should like to see them, too, but we can't have everything at once. We have these dear friends now and hope to have the other and still dearer ones next spring."

"Milly, you know you offered to hear my lessons while we are here, but Cousin Horace says he will teach me along with Elsie, if I like."

"That is very kind, and I think it will be much nicer for you because he knows very much more than I do and how to impart his knowledge. And you will enjoy having a companion in your studies, especially so sweet a one as Elsie.

"Yes, and she says it will be pleasanter for her. Then it will save your some trouble, too. We're to begin next Monday morning. Milly, don't you like Mr. Travilla?"

"Yes, very much, and I love his mother dearly. She wants us to spend part of our time with them at Ion. And we must visit Roselands, too."

"I'd rather stay here."

"Of course, the greater portion of the winter will be spent here. Perhaps a week at each of the other places will be enough."

The visitors for the day had all gone, and when Rose went to the nursery, Mildred to her room, and Annis presently slipped away to follow her sister, while Dr. Landreth seemed buried in a book, Mr. Dinsmore said to Elsie, "Come with me, daughter," and led the way to his private study.

"Oh, it's nice to be here alone with you again, papa!" she exclaimed as he sat down and drew her to his knee.

"Yes, we don't spend so much time alone together nowadays as has been our custom," he said, drawing her closer to him. "But I hope my little girl is enjoying herself?"

"Oh, yes indeed, papa! I think Annis is the very nicest little friend I've ever had."

"She ought to be, considering how thoroughly well she has been brought up. But I brought you in here to teach you a lesson."

Elsie opened her eyes wide in surprise. "Why, papa, I thought you said I was to have a holiday all week, and this is only Friday evening!"

"That's a fact!" he said, as if she had brought to his recollection something he had forgotten, "and as I am particular about keeping my promises, I shall not insist on teaching you the intended lesson. We will leave it until next week, if you prefer that."

She considered a moment, then said, "Papa, I will learn it now, if you please."

"I think you will not regret your decision," he answered with a gratified look. Then turning to his writing desk, which was close at hand, he took from it a thin paper covered book, and opening it showed her that the leaves were composed of blank forms of checks.

"The lesson I want to teach you," he said, "is how to fill these up properly. I have placed one thousand dollars in the bank to your credit, and this book is for your use so that you may draw out the money as you want it."

She looked surprised, pleased, and yet a little puzzled.

"You are very kind, papa," she said, "but you give me so much pocket money that I never should know what use to make of it all if I couldn't give it away."

"But you enjoy giving, and I am very glad you do. At Christmastime, you always need extra money for that purpose, and Christmas will be coming again some weeks hence. Will you not wish to give some handsome presents to these cousins here and enjoy making up a Christmas box for those in Indiana?"

"Oh, papa, what a nice idea!" she cried, clapping her hands. "And may I spend all that thousand dollars?"

"Perhaps; we will see about it. Now for the lesson."

He showed her how to fill up the the blank spaces with the number, date, amount, and where to sign her name, giving a simple and clear explanation of the why and wherefore of it all. Then he let her practice on several of the forms, till she grew quite proficient.

She was greatly pleased and interested. "It's very nice, papa! How kind you are to teach me!"

"I want as early as possible to make you capable of managing your own business affairs," he said, stroking her hair, "so that if I should be taken from you—"

"Oh, papa," she interrupted, her eyes filling with sudden tears, "don't talk about that! How could I ever bear it!"

"My child," he said with a tender caress, "I am in perfect health and, coming of a long-lived stock, seem as likely to live to extreme old age as anyone I know. But life is uncertain to us all, and it is the part of wisdom to try to be prepared for any event. You inherit large wealth from your mother, but riches, as the Bible tells us, take wings and fly away—and are especially apt to do so with a woman who knows little or nothing about business.

"I would not have you at the mercy of sharpers and fortune hunters, so I am determined not to allow you to grow up either too lazy or too ignorant to take care of your own affairs. I shall teach you how to write an order, a receipt for money, to make out a bill, and so on. But this lesson will do for today."

"Now these forms you have filled out must be destroyed," he went on, tearing them up and throwing the fragments into the fire as he spoke. "Do you understand why?"

"No, sir."

"Because, bearing your signature, they would be honored at the bank where you have money on deposit; that is, anyone getting hold of and presenting them at the bank would be paid the sums named in them out of your money, and then you would lose just that amount. So, if you want to give or pay money to anybody, your check on a bank where you have money deposited will answer the same purpose as the cash, provided it be not drawn for a larger sum than you have there. Do you understand it all now?"

"Yes, papa, I think I do. May I tell Annis about it?"

"If you wish," he said with a smile. "Annis is worthy of all confidence. You may take the checkbook and go over your lesson to her. It will help to impress it on your memory."

"Oh, thank you, sir!" she said, and away she ran in search of her cousin.

Annis was still in Mildred's room, chatting with her sister and playing with the baby.

She opened the door in answer to Elsie's gentle rap.

"Oh, I'm so glad it's you! she said. "Come in, won't you?"

"Am I not intruding?" asked Elsie.

"No, no, dear child!" replied Mildred, "Annis and I were just wishing for your company."

"Oh, I am glad you wanted me," said the little girl, taking a low chair by Mildred's side. "I should have come sooner, but I've been with papa, learning such a nice lesson!" And opening her checkbook, she went on to tell all about it, for she felt sure he would not object to having Mildred hear it as well as Annis.

Both seemed much interested and said they thought it a very nice lesson indeed, Annis adding, "And very delightful to have so much money where you can get it whenever you want it."

"Yes," Elsie said, "but I don't believe papa meant that I could ever take any of it out without asking his permission. And I always have to keep an account to show him what I have done with every cent he has given me to spend."

"That must be a great deal of trouble!" Annis remarked with a slight shrug of her shoulders.

"But an excellent lesson, too," Mildred said, smiling into Elsie's bright, happy face.

"Yes, cousin, papa always knows and does the very best thing for me," the little girl responded with a look of perfect content.

At breakfast next morning, the gentlemen announced that business called them to the city and invited both the ladies and the little girls to drive in with them.

The latter joyfully accepted, but the ladies preferred a quiet day at home.

"Now, little girls," Mr. Dinsmore said, as they rose from the table, "the carriage will be at the door in half an hour, and I should like you to be ready by that time. But, Elsie, I want you in the study for a little while the first thing."

He walked away in that direction as he spoke, and she tripped merrily after him.

"I'm going to the bank to get a check cashed. Would you like to do the same?" he asked, turning to her with a kind, fatherly smile as he opened his writing desk.

"Yes, papa. You will go with me and show me just what to do?"

"Of course, my daughter. If I thought there was any danger of your going there without me for years to come, I should very politely forbid it."

"Ah," she said, with a contented little laugh, "I was pretty sure you didn't mean to let me get out some of that money just whenever I pleased."

"No, you are quite too young for such latitude

as that. Now sit down here and let me see how well you remember yesterday's lesson." he said, dipping a pen into the ink and putting it into her hand as she took the designated seat.

"How much money shall I write it for, papa?" she asked.

"Any sum you please not over fifty dollars."

"I think twenty-five will do," she said, and drew the check correctly for that amount.

"Very nicely done, daughter," he said in a pleased tone. "Now fold it and put it into your purse."

"What will you have me wear, papa?"

"The blue velvet suit, unless you prefer some other equally suitable to the occasion."

"All I care about it is to please my papa," she said, smiling up at him.

"That being the case, it is well that papa has good taste, isn't it?" he said sportively, stroking her hair and stooping to touch his lips to the pure white forehead. "Now run away and tell Aunt Chloe to dress you immediately."

"Yes, sir. It won't take long, because it is only to change my dress and put on hat, coat, and gloves."

Annis, now quite ready excepting her gloves, was in her own room, the door of communication with Elsie's apartments open as usual. Mildred, too, was there superintending her little sister's preparations.

"Is mammy here!" Elsie asked, looking in. "Oh, no, I see she is not. I'll have to ring for her because there is no time to wait, and I'm sorry, for I'm afraid she is eating her breakfast."

"Let me help you instead," said Mildred. "You see, I have quite finished with Annis."

"I don't like to trouble you, Cousin Milly."

"It will be no trouble, dear, but a pleasure. And I should like to make some small return to your good mammy for the help she gives Annis with her dressing."

So Elsie accepted with thanks, adding merrily, "Won't mammy be astonished! She thinks nobody can dress me but herself."

While the dressing was going on, Elsie told with glee what she had been doing in the study and that she was to be taken to the bank to present the check there herself.

Annis was greatly interested. "I hope I can go along and see you do it," she said. "But won't you feel a little frightened?"

"Not with papa close beside me."

"That makes all the difference in the world, doesn't it dear?" Mildred said, finishing her labors with a kiss upon the round, rosy cheek.

"Me, too, Milly," Annis said, holding up her face. "Now goodbye, and take good care of my little nephew while I'm gone."

"Yes. Run away now and don't keep the gentlemen waiting. The carriage has just driven round to the side entrance."

"Good girls! You should have a medal for punctuality," Dr. Landreth remarked, meeting them on the veranda.

"And for bright, happy faces," added Mr. Dinsmore, handing them into the carriage.

"I don't think little girls who have everything in

the world to make them happy deserve much credit for that, Cousin Horace," said Annis.

"Well, perhaps not, but there are people who can always find something to growl or fret about."

The little girls were very merry during the drive, and neither gentleman showed the slightest inclination to check their mirthfulness. But for that, there was no occasion, since there was not the least approach to rudeness in any of its manifestations.

On reaching the city, they drove directly to the bank in which Mr. Dinsmore and Elsie were depositors. They all went in together, and Annis looked on with great interest while Elsie handed in her check, received the money, and counted it under her father's supervision.

They spent some hours in the city, sightseeing and shopping, and returned home to a late dinner. The children rather weary but were in fine spirits and full of merry talk about all they had seen and done.

In the meanwhile, the two ladies had found equal enjoyment at home, spending the day very quietly in Rose's boudoir, each busy in the fashioning of a dainty garment for her baby-boy and talking together as they worked.

Both young—though Mildred was Rose's senior by several years—both happily married, tender mothers, highly cultivated women, earnest Christians, they soon discovered that they had very much in common.

Naturally, their talk was at first of the pretty work with which their hands were busied, then of the little ones for whose adornment it was intended, then of their husbands and the days of their courtship. Each already had some slight knowledge of the other's experience but now became more fully acquainted with it. Mildred told something of her hard trial in the long years of doubt and uncertainty while she knew not where her beloved wanderer was, and of the support and comfort she found in the presence and love of One nearer and dearer still.

Rose had not yet known any trial more severe than the parting from parents, brothers and sisters, and the loved home of her childhood, but she also could talk of sweet experiences of that "Love divine all love excelling."

"Then they that feared the Lord spake often one to another: and the Lord hearkened, and heard it, and a book of remembrance was written before Him for them that feared the Lord, and that thought upon His name. And they shall be mine, saith the Lord of hosts, in that day when I make up my jewels; and I will spare them, as a man spareth his own son that serveth him."

CHAPTER XII

I want a sweet sense of Thy pardoning love,
That my manifold sins are forgiven;
That Christ as my Advocate pleadeth above,
That my name is recorded in Heaven.

"WELL, ANNIS, WILL you take a riding lesson this afternoon?" asked Mr. Dinsmore as they left the dinner table. Then, seeing the little girl hesitate in her reply, he added, "Ah, I think you are tired and would prefer a nap."

"Yes, sir, I believe I should, if—" and again she hesitated.

"If I will not feel hurt?" he asked with a smile. "No, not in the least. And I advise Elsie to try a siesta too. Then we older people shall have two bright little girls to help our enjoyment of the evening."

Elsie thought it a very nice plan, and the two went away together to carry it out.

"Your prescription seems to have worked well, Dinsmore," was Dr. Landreth's smiling remark as the two young faces showed themselves in the parlor shortly before tea, rosy, bright, and beaming with health and happiness.

"Yes, I have found there is no other restorer of

wearied nature equal to restful sleep," Mr. Dinsmore said, regarding his little girl with his wonted look of proud, fond, fatherly affection. "Are you quite rested, daughter?" he asked, drawing her to his side.

"Yes, sir, I don't believe I shall need any moe sleep till after ten o'clock tonight," she answered, looking straight into his eyes with an arch, sweet smile.

"Ah," he said with amusement, "quite an adroit way of putting a request to be allowed to stay up beyond the regular hour for retiring. Well, we'll see about it when the time comes."

"And Elsie will be contented with papa's decision, whatever it may be," added Rose, smiling affectionately upon the little girl.

"Are you not fond of going to bed early, Elsie?" asked the doctor.

"Yes, sir, generally. But I think it is very nice to stay up a little later sometimes, when papa is willing and I'm not sleepy."

"And," remarked Annis, "when the grown-up folks are playing games or talking in a very interesting way, it does seem hard for little folks to have to go away and leave it all."

"Yes," said Mildred, "I can remember that I felt it so when I was a child. Yet I mean to train my boy to go to his bed at a regular and early hour, for I am convinced that it will be for his good."

"I hope everybody wants to play with letters again tonight," remarked Annis, "because I've hunted up some very hard words for Cousin Horace and Brother Charlie to make out."

"You are not going to bestow all your favors upon them, I hope," Rose said playfully.

The older people being in an amiable mood, the wishes of both little girls were gratified to some extent, the greater part of the evening being spent in word-making, and Elsie permitted to stay up half an hour beyond her regular bedtime.

Sunday always passed very quickly at the Oaks. The master and mistress, having a supreme regard for the sacredness of the day, gave no entertainments and allowed no unnecessary work in the house or on the plantation. It was a time of peaceful Sabbath rest.

The church to which the family belonged was some miles distant, but nothing except sickness or extremely inclement weather ever keep them at home from the morning service—the only one held there.

The afternoon and evening were also profitably spent in studying the Scriptures for themselves and in imparting their teachings to the ignorant about them.

The first Sunday after the arrival of the cousins from Pleasant Plains was clear and bright. The ladies and little girls drove to church in the family carriage, the gentlemen accompanying them on horseback.

The short ride through beautiful country in the bright sunlight and pure, bracing autumn air was a pleasant one for all. To Annis, it had the charm of novelty; to Dr. Landreth and Mildred, that of agreeable association. How often they had traversed that road together or met in the little church during the winter she had spent at Roselands years ago!

The Roselands family was represented today by Mrs. Dinsmore, Adelaide, and Lora. Mr. Travilla and his mother, from Ion, were present at the service also, and at its close, there was a little chat among them all in the vestibule of the church—an exchange of kindly greetings and inquiries before the ladies were handed into their carriages and the gentlemen mounted their steeds for the homeward trip.

"How do you spend the rest of the day, Elsie?" Annis asked when they found themselves again in Elsie's pretty boudoir.

"Part of it in teaching the servants about Jesus and the way to heaven. Papa and mamma have classes of the grown-ups, and I have one of the little boys and girls. I tell them Bible stories, sometimes from the Old Testament and sometimes from the New. I have a simple little catechism, too, that I teach them by asking the questions and making them repeat the answers after me," Elsie replied, with an animation of look and tone which showed that she felt greatly interested in her work.

"I like best of all to talk to them about the wonderful love of Jesus," she went on, "how he left that beautiful heaven and came down to our world, and labored and suffered and died the cruel death on the cross, keeping God's holy law for us and bearing the penalty of our sins, and how he rose again and ascended to heaven and ever lives there to make intercession for us. Oh, Annis, isn't it the sweetest story?"

Tears were trembling in the soft eyes, and Annis, putting her arms about her, said, "What a good little Christian you are, Elsie! I wish I were one, too."

"Oh, I'm not at all good, Annis," answered the little girl with earnest sincerity, "but I do love Jesus. Don't you?"

"I'm not sure. I do try to do right, but I so often do wrong that I'm afraid I'm not a Christian."

"But, oh, Annis, Christians are not people who never do wrong, but they are those who trust only in the blood and merits of Jesus Christ, who expect to be saved because of what he has done and suffered, and who long and strive to be good and holy because they love him and want to please him and be like him. Not because they expect to be saved by being good. Don't you remember? The Bible says, 'There is none that doeth good, no, not one.' 'There is not a just man upon earth, that doeth good, and sinneth not.'"

"Yes, I remember that, and that even the Apostle Paul said he couldn't do the good he wanted to and couldn't help doing the evil he didn't want to." Annis said thoughtfully. "I see the difference is that Christians hate sin and want to be free from it because God hates it and it is dishonoring to Him, and sinners love it and would only leave it off for fear of punishment."

"Yes, you know the Bible says, 'Be ye therefore followers of God as dear children!' Oh, I think I understand what that means! Because, loving my dear papa so much, and feeling so sure that I am a very dear child to him, I almost always find it a real pleasure to obey him."

"Yes, and I can understand it for the same reason. Isn't it a sweet text?"

"Yes indeed! And, oh how many others there are that are 'sweeter than honey and the honey-comb,' as the Psalmist says," Elsie exclaimed, taking up her Bible and turning its pages.

"May I be with you while you talk to your little scholars?" asked Annis.

"Oh, yes, if you wish, and perhaps you may like to teach some of them yourself."

"Well, maybe," Annis answered, and just then the call to dinner came.

At the table, Dr. Landreth asked Mr. Dinsmore the same question which Elsie had answered to Annis: "How do you spend the rest of the day here? I understand there is no afternoon or evening service near enough for us to attend."

"No, there is not," replied Mr. Dinsmore, who went on to tell of the afternoon instruction to the servants.

"After that," said he, "we usually fill up the time with suitable reading, and I hear Elsie recite her catechism, passages of Scripture, and perhaps a hymn or two. Most of our evening is usually spent in the study of the Word—a Bible reading in which the three of us take part—and we are very apt to have some sacred music after that. Will you and Mildred and Annis join us in such exercises tonight?"

The invitation was accepted with pleasure by all three.

"What subject shall we take up tonight?" asked Mr. Dinsmore as they gathered about the center table after tea with Bibles, Concordance, and Bible Textbook.

"Christ a living Saviour," suggested Mildred, "living still in both his divine and his human nature."

"There could not be a sweeter theme," said Rose. "'Who is he that condemneth? It is Christ that died, yea, rather, that is risen again; who is even at the right hand of God, who also maketh intercession for us.'"

"I should like nothing better," said the doctor.

"Nor I," added Mr. Dinsmore. "I have often thought that while we cannot dwell too much upon the theme of Christ's life on earth and atoning sacrifice—his sufferings and death in our stead—we do not think and talk enough of his resurrection and ascension into heaven, of his mediatorial work there. Here in Hebrews we are told, 'This man, because he continueth ever, hath an unchangeable priesthood. Wherefore he is able also to save them to the uttermost that come unto God by him, seeing he ever liveth to make intercession for them.'"

"Yes," said Mildred, "I have thought much about it since a talk I had some time ago with a gentleman friend who is, I believe, a true Christian, yet who surprised me greatly by remarking that he had always thought Christ's body ceased to exist after his death because—so it seemed to him—he had no further use for it."

"What a very strange and unscriptural idea!" exclaimed Rose. "Why, the Bible seems to me to teach that belief in the resurrection of Christ is necessary to salvation. 'If thou shalt confess with thy mouth the Lord Jesus, and shalt believe in thine heart that God hath raised Him from the dead, thou shalt be saved.' And it was His human body that died, was buried, and rose again."

"What did your friend think became of it?" queried the doctor. "Matter is indestructible, and besides, we are told that he saw no corruption."

"Yes, in several passages. Here is one—Acts 13, beginning with verse 29," said Mildred, who read aloud: "'And when they had fulfilled all that was written of him, they took him down from the tree, and laid him in a sepulcher; but God raised him from the dead: and he was seen many days of them which came up with him from Galilee to Jerusalem, who are his witnesses unto the people. And we declare unto you glad tidings, how that the promise which was made unto the fathers, God hath fulfilled the same unto us their children, in that he hath raised up Jesus again; as it is also written in the second psalm, Thou art my Son, this day have I begotten thee. And as concerning that he raised him up from the dead, now no more to return to corruption, he said on this wise, I will give you the sure mercies of David. Wherefore he saith also in another psalm, Thou shalt not suffer thine Holy One to see corruption. For David, after he had served his own generation by the will of God, fell on sleep, and was laid unto his fathers, and saw corruption: But he, whom God raised again, saw no corruption.'"

"There we have the whole thing," remarked her husband, "and as far as proof is concerned, need look no farther."

"But, oh, mayn't we go on and hunt out other passages?" asked Elsie eagerly.

"What have you there?" asked her father, for her Bible was open in her hand.

"The fifteenth chapter of first Corinthians, beginning with the third verse, papa: 'For I delivered unto you first of all that which I also received, how that Christ died for our sins according to the Scriptures; and that he was seen of Cephas, then of the twelve: After that he was seen of above five hundred brethren at once: of whom the greater part remain unto this present, but some are fallen asleep. After that he was seen of James, then of all the apostles. And last of all he was seen of me also, as of one born out of due time.'"

"Does Paul tell there of every time that the risen Saviour was seen and recognized by those who had known him before his death?" asked Mr. Dinsmore.

"Oh, no indeed, papa! Mary Magdalene saw him in the garden just after he had risen, and then—But, Annis, don't you want to tell of the others?"

Annis looked her thanks and added, "The two who were walking into the country; the disciples who had met together in the upper room when

Thomas wasn't with them, and afterward when he was with them; Peter and John and some of the others when they were out in a boat fishing."

Annis paused, and Mildred proposed that each passage bearing on the subject should be sought out and read aloud, all taking turns.

"Not a link wanting in the chain of evidence," remarked Mr. Dinsmore as they finished with these words from the account of the martyrdom of Stephen: "'But he, being full of the Holy Ghost, looked up steadfastly into heaven and saw the glory of God, and Jesus standing on the right hand of God, and said, Behold, I see the heavens opened, and the Son of man standing on the right hand of God,'—we have just read, 'that he died, was buried, rose from the grave, ascended into heaven and there remains at God's right hand.'"

"Where he ever liveth to make intercession for us," added Rose softly, a glad light in her sweet blue eyes.

Then Mildred read aloud from her open Bible, "'Seeing then that we have a great high priest, that is passed into the heavens, Jesus, the Son of God, let us hold fast our profession. For we have not a high priest which cannot be touched with the feeling of our infirmities; but was in all points tempted like as we are, yet without sin.'"

CHAPTER XIII

Wake, slumberer! morning's golden hours
Are speeding fast away;
The sun has waked the opening flowers,
To greet the new-born day.

—EPES SARGENT

ELSIE STIRRED IN her sleep, half dreamily conscious that it was near her usual hour for rising, then someone bent over her and a kiss on the lips awoke her fully.

"Papa!" she cried softly, looking up into his face with her now wide-open, beautiful eyes. Then, putting her arm round his neck, she drew him down closer and returned his caress with a whispered "Good morning, my own dear papa."

"Good morning, my darling," he said. "Do you feel well and bright and as if a gallop before breakfast with your father would be enjoyable?"

"Oh, yes, yes indeed, papa!" she cried, starting up, with a face full of delight.

"Well, then, get up at once. Let Aunt Chloe dress you in your riding habit and give you a glass of good rich milk, and we will go. Annis seems to be still sleeping. Don't make any noise

118

to disturb her, and after breakfast you and she can take a short drive in the phaeton."

"I wish mamma was going with us," Elsie said as her father assisted her to mount her pony.

"It would be very pleasant to have her company," he answered, "but she prefers another nap, having lost sleep during the night by the babe's wakefulness.

"Annis is getting another nap, too," Elsie remarked. "I peeped in at her just before I left my rooms."

"Ah! Then I hope she will not miss you."

"Oh, let us have a brisk ride, won't you, papa?" she asked as they passed out of the grounds into the highway.

"I see no objection," he returned, smiling indulgently upon her, and away they flew.

Elsie had not been long gone when Annis awoke. She lay still for a little, thinking. She remembered that today she was to begin lessons with her Cousin Horace, and the prospect was not altogether pleasant. She feared he would think her a dull scholar and not so far advanced in her studies as she ought to be.

Then it occurred to her that it was time to get up. The fire had been attended to and the room was very pleasantly warm. She threw back the covers and stepped out upon the thick, soft carpet.

"Ah, is you gettin' up, honey?" asked Aunt Chloe, peering in at the half-open door. "I'se done dressin' my chile, and now I kin help you, ef you's willin'."

"Thank you, auntie, I'd be very glad to have you do up my hair and hook my dress. But where is Elsie? It is so quiet in there that I thought she was still asleep."

"Yah, yah!" laughed the old nurse. "Miss Elsie, she done gone ridin' wid Massa Horace."

"Why, dear me, I must be shamefully late!" exclaimed Annis in dismay as she began dressing in great haste.

"No, missy, you's got plenty time. Dey's early, dat's all."

Much relieved by the assurance, Annis went on with her dressing rather more leisurely.

She had finished and was sitting in an easy chair beside the fire reading her Bible when Elsie returned from the gallop and came in holding up the skirt of her habit with one hand and carrying in the other a little gold-mounted riding whip. She was radiant with health and happiness, her eyes shining and a lovely color in her cheeks.

"Good morning, Annis dear," she said, running to her cousin with an offered kiss. "Please excuse me for leaving you, but you seemed to be having a very nice nap, and papa wanted me to take a short ride with him before breakfast."

"I don't see any call for excuse," returned Annis with good humor. "I'm glad you went, for I'm sure it has done you good," she added, gazing admiringly into her dressing room. "Please, mammy, make me ready for breakfast as fast as you can, or I shall not have much time with papa," she said to Aunt Chloe, who was waiting with a pretty morning dress and sash laid out in readiness.

"Yes, honey darlin', I'se hab you ready in less dan no time," she responded, beginning to remove the riding hat and habit as she spoke.

Her preparations complete, Elsie hastened, Bible in hand, to her father's study. She found him seated with his Bible open before him.

"I hope I have not kept you waiting long, papa," she said, taking her accustomed seat upon his knee.

"No, daughter, you have been very prompt," he replied, tenderly enfolding her with his arm. "Your ride has not wearied you?"

"Oh, no, sir. I am not tired at all."

They read a few verses, talked together of the truth taught in them, then knelt while Mr. Dinsmore offered a short prayer. After that, she resumed her seat upon his knee until the call to breakfast.

"You have not forgotten that lessons are to be begun again today?" he said interrogatively, taking the small white hands in his and softly patting and stroking them as he spoke.

"No, sir, and I intend to try to be very industrious, to make up for lost time."

"That is right, and I don't expect to hear a word of grumbling over the Latin lesson."

"Papa," she exclaimed energetically, "if you do, I ought to be punished!"

"In what way?" he asked with unmoved gravity, though there was a twinkle of amusement in his eye.

"Ah, that of course would be for you to decide, papa," she said, giving him a hug and kiss.

"Well, I advise you not to give me the opportunity. Have you thought what you would like to send as Christmas gifts to your cousins at Pleasant Plains?"

"No, sir."

"Better talk it over with mamma."

"And you, papa. I do think you always know better how to please with presents than anybody else."

"Oh, my child," he said, laughing, "if I swallowed all your loving flattery, what a conceited creature I should become! Perhaps you can, in talking with Mildred and Annis, get an idea of what would best please the others. Ah, there is the call to breakfast," he said, and gently putting her off his knee, he rose, took her hand in his, and led her to the breakfast room.

As soon as the meal and family worship were over, the little girls had their drive. Annis enjoyed it exceedingly, and Elsie nearly as much.

By the time they had returned and taken off their wraps, the hour for study had arrived.

Elsie took out her books and showed Annis her lessons for the day. Seating themselves side by side, the two began their tasks together.

They were about equally advanced in their studies and could work together to advantage, as Mr. Dinsmore discovered on hearing the recitations and examining Annis as to her acquirements.

"Papa," said Elsie, "I think it very nice and enjoyable to have company in studying and reciting, and I guess I shall learn all the faster for it."

"I hope so, daughter, but I do not like that use

of the word 'guess'—in the sense of expect, think, suppose, presume, conjecture, believe. Don't use it in that way again."

"I'm afraid she has learned it from me, Cousin Horace," Annis said ingenuously. "It's a bad habit of mine that father and mother both dislike. I have tried to break myself of it, and I mean to try harder after this."

"I'll try to remember not to use it anymore, papa," said Elsie. "But please tell me, is it quite incorrect or only inelegant?"

"It is quite incorrect when one guesses about things well known. It is only inelegant when used in the sense of conjecture, divine, surmise, suppose, believe, or think concerning something we do not know. Any one of these words seems to me preferable. The use of 'guess' in those senses is often spoken of as an Americanism but unjustly, as it has been so used by Milton, Locke, Shakespeare, and other prominent English writers."

"I am glad to know that," said Annis. "Cousin Horace, I think I shall like you as a tutor very much indeed."

"You don't guess so?" he said with a smile. "Well, what do you say to taking a riding lesson now?"

"Oh, that I should like it greatly, if it will not trouble you or take too much of your time."

"No, I can spare time for that and also for a walk with my two pupils," he said, laying a hand caressingly on Elsie's head as she stood at his side. "How soon can you be ready?"

"Oh, directly, papa," was Elsie's answer, while Annis answered, "In two minutes, cousin."

"I haven't seen Milly since breakfast!" exclaimed Annis, tripping along by Mr. Dinsmore's side. "I wonder if she went into the city to shop?"

"No," he answered, "she and my wife were returning their calls this morning. I was invited to accompany them and should have enjoyed doing so had not business detained me at home."

"Oh, papa, what a pity!" said Elsie. "Couldn't you have heard our lessons this afternoon?"

"That would have been possible but not best, I thought. Besides, I had other matters, connected with the work on the plantation, claiming my attention. Is Mildred wanting to go to the city to shop, Annis?"

"Yes, sir," replied the little girl, her whole face lighting up with pleasure. "We are going to make up a Christmas box for the folks at home, and Milly says it must start soon to get there in time. The journey is so long, you know. We bought some things in Philadelphia but hadn't time to buy all we wanted."

"May I ask what sort of things they were?" he queried in a playful tone.

"Oh, yes indeed, Cousin Horace. We bought gloves, handkerchiefs, ribbons, and laces for mother and the girls, neckties and handkerchiefs for the boys and father, and some beautiful coral and gold armlets for little Stuart Ormsby— Zillah's baby, you know—and some lovely fine white material for dresses for him, and beautiful needlework to trim them with."

"Thank you for telling me," Mr. Dinsmore said,

"and I should be very glad to learn of some other things you and Mildred think would please them, for Elsie and I must beg leave to have a share in this pleasant business. Must we not, daughter?"

"Oh, yes indeed," she cried with enthusiasm. "It will be a very great pleasure! I want to remember each one with some nice gift."

"You are both very kind," Annis answered with a pleased look. "We all think at home there never were such kind relations as our Dinsmore uncle and cousins."

"My father is the soul of generosity," Mr. Dinsmore remarked. "But those to whom God has entrusted such abundant means as he has to Elsie and myself, so that giving does not involve much, if any self-denial, do not deserve any great amount of credit for it, especially when they find it the most enjoyable way of using their money."

Walk and riding lesson over, they returned to the house.

It was time to dress for dinner. That attended to, the little girls sought the ladies in Mrs. Dinsmore's boudoir, where they sat in dinner dress but busy with their fancy work.

The gentlemen were there too, chatting with their wives and playing with their baby boys.

The moment little Horace caught sight of his sister, he held out his arms to her with a crow of delight, for he was already very fond of her.

Hastening to her father's side, she said in her most coaxing tones, "Oh, papa, may I take him?"

"Sit down in that low chair, and I will put him on your lap," he answered.

"Oh, thank you, sir," she said, gladly complying with the condition.

"Annis," said the doctor, "I hear you are on your way to become an accomplished horsewoman."

"In as fair a way as having the best of teachers can make me."

"And a good little pony to learn on," added Elsie.

"Yes indeed," assented Annis. "Mildred," she said, turning to her sister, "you didn't go shopping today?"

"No, we thought best to pay our calls first, and that took all the morning. We hope, though, to shop tomorrow."

"Cousin Horace, will you allow your pupils to have a share in the shopping?" asked Annis half laughingly, turning to Mr. Dinsmore as she spoke.

"If the lessons have first been recited correctly," he replied. "Mildred, will you allow me a share in that shopping?"

"Your company is always agreeable, Cousin Horace."

"But he means more than that," Annis said gleefully. "He and Elsie want to buy things for our box too."

"And so you told them about it, though I begged you not to do so?" Mildred returned, reproachfully.

"You are not to blame her," remarked Mr. Dinsmore. "It was no fault of hers. I wormed it out of her. But I don't see, Milly, why you should wish to deprive us of the pleasure of taking part in such work?"

"Just because you and Elsie are both too generous and must have plenty of other uses for your money."

"My dear little lady," he answered smilingly, "are not we the best judges of that?"

"Come, Milly, be generous and don't try to keep your pleasure all to yourself," her husband said, standing by her side and looking down at her with laughing, admiring eyes.

"I trust you don't really think I need that admonition, my dear," she responded, lifting to his face eyes brimming with confiding affection.

CHAPTER XIV

Industry—
To meditate, to plan, resolve, perform,
Which in itself is good—as surely brings
Beware of good, no matter what be done.

—POLLOCK

IT WAS DECIDED that the box for Pleasant Plains must start within a week, so there was no time to be lost in getting it ready.

Shortly after leaving the tea table, the two little girls held a whispered consultation, the result of which was that they stole quietly away to Elsie's boudoir and set to work with zeal and determination upon the morrow's lessons.

It was a lovely moonlight evening, and a carriage load of company, and two or three gentlemen on horseback, arriving just as they left the parlor, prevented them from being missed for a couple of hours.

Then, the visitors having taken leave, the elder members of the family began to wonder what had become of the children, and presently Mr. Dinsmore went in search of them.

"Papa," cried Elsie, looking up from her book as he entered the boudoir, "we have learned our lessons for tomorrow. Won't you hear them now and let us go to the city in the morning with mamma and Cousin Mildred?"

"I will hear the recitations, and if I find them satisfactory, shall certainly consider you deserving of the favor you ask," he replied, seating himself and taking the book she held out to him.

"You have both done extremely well, and if nothing happens to prevent, shall go the city with the ladies tomorrow," he said when the last lesson had been recited.

Both the young faces were full of delight.

"Thank you, Cousin Horace," said Annis.

"Thank you, my dear, kind father," Elsie said, seating herself on his knee and giving him a hug and kiss. "Annis says father always, and it sounds so nice. May I say it too? I mean would you like me to, papa?"

"Address me by whichever title pleases you best, my darling. Both are very sweet to my ear coming from your lips," he said, holding her close. "But come now, we must return to our friends. It is time for prayers."

After prayers, Annis followed Mildred to her rooms to tell how her evening and Elsie's had been spent and to talk about the purchases to be made on the morrow.

Mildred sympathized fully with her little sister's pleasure, praised her industry, and gave patient attention to the other matters, and advice in regard to them.

"I don't think we can quite decide what will be best for you to buy till we see the pretty things in the stores," she said at length. "And now, dear child, I think it is about time for you to be getting ready for bed."

"Yes, I suppose it is. Oh, Milly, I do love you so! You are just like a mother to me, now while we are away from our own dear mother," Annis said, giving and receiving a close and tender embrace.

Dr. Landreth came in at that moment and as the two released each other said, "Now, Annis, isn't it my turn? I've been your brother for a good while, and you have never given me a hug yet."

"I never hug gentlemen, except my father and brothers," she returned, coloring and edging away from him.

"Of course not; but don't you acknowledge me as your brother?"

"I think you are a very nice brother," she said, remembering his many acts of kindness, "but not—"

"Not the sort you like to hug, eh? Then you oughtn't to hug Mildred, because she and I are one."

"I don't think so," she said, laughing and shaking her head, "and I have let you hug me once or twice."

"Ah, but that's another thing! See here, I'll give you this if you'll pay for it with such a hug as you gave Milly just now." And he held up a gold double-eagle coin.

Annis's eyes sparkled. "That's twenty dollars, isn't it?"

"Yes."

"I'd like to have it, but if it's to be a gift you can't ask pay for it."

"True enough," he said, tossing it up and catching it again. "Well, how am I to contrive to get what I want?"

"If you really want it so much, Brother Charlie, you shall have it for nothing because I am 'most as fond of you as if you were my very own brother," she said, permitting him to catch her in his arms and putting hers about his neck.

"That's right," he said, kissing her on both cheeks. "And now, as I'm not to be outdone in generosity, you shall have the gold piece as a free gift."

He put it into her hand, and with a half-breathless "Oh, thank you. I never was so rich before!" and a merry good night to him and Mildred, too, she hurried away, eager to tell Elsie of her good fortune.

"It was worth twenty dollars just to see her delight," he remarked to his wife. "Don't you think so, Milly?"

"Yes! How kind and generous you are, my dear husband."

As the cousins left the parlor, Elsie drew out her watch, glanced at it, then gave her father a wistful, pleading look.

He smiled and held out his hand. "Yes, it is your bedtime I know, but a little girl who has been so industrious all evening I think deserves a little indulgence."

She was on his knee and he was caressing her before the sentence was finished.

"And papa is very glad of a good excuse to indulge her and himself at the same time," Rose said, regarding the two with a look of mingled amusement and satisfaction.

"Quite true, mamma," Mr. Dinsmore returned, caressing Elsie again and again, "but I hardly expected you to be so keen-eyed as to see through my little subterfuge, so very small a one that in fact I was hardly aware of it myself."

"But what has Elsie been so busy about, if I may know?"

"Oh, yes, mamma, of course you may. I have only been learning and reciting my lessons—Annis and I—so that we might go with you and Cousin Mildred in the morning. And papa says we may if nothing happens to prevent."

"Such, for instance, as a disinclination for your company on the part of your mother and cousin."

"No danger of that impediment," remarked Rose with an affectionate look at her little step-daughter. "I can answer for myself and Mildred, too, that we shall be glad to have them with us."

"Thank you, dear mamma," said Elsie. "Papa, how much may I spend on the presents for the cousins?"

"A hundred dollars, if you wish. What do you think of buying?"

"I don't know, sir. Mamma, can you suggest something?"

"Laces, ribbons, gloves, handkerchiefs—a lady can hardly have too many of any of those."

"Or of books of the right sort," added Mr. Dinsmore, "or of ornaments for the hair and dress. A handsome party fan makes a nice present, too. But we need not decide fully until we see what the merchants have. It is sufficient for the present to have an idea of what we want. And now it is high time for my little daughter to go to bed. Good night, my darling."

Aunt Chloe's busy hands were preparing her nursling for bed when Annis came dancing in, holding up her double eagle.

"See, Elsie, what Brother Charlie has just given me! Wasn't he kind, and isn't it pretty? I never before had a larger gold piece than a quarter eagle. It's so bright and new, it seems too pretty to spend, but I mean to spend it tomorrow, for it will buy ever so many nice things for mother and the rest."

"It's a beauty!" Elsie said, taking it in her hand for a moment. "I remember papa gave me one three years ago when I was starting off to buy Christmas gifts, and I was so glad, for my purse wasn't nearly so full as I wished it was."

"But this year you have a bank to fill it from," laughed Annis. "Oh, Elsie, I do think that must be ever so nice!"

"But it doesn't make much difference when you can't get any out without leave," Elsie responded with a smile and a little shake of her pretty head. "I hadn't told papa I wanted more money that time and didn't expect it in the least, because he had given me fifty dollars extra for Christmas just a few weeks before. But somehow papa always seems to know what I want. And he is sure to give it to me if he thinks it good for me to have it."

"Yes, he's a very nice father, and so is mine," Annis said, "though he can't afford to give me so much money—partly, I guess, because he has 'most as many children as the old woman that lived in a shoe. Oh, dear! I forgot I wasn't going to say 'guess' any more, Elsie. I'm afraid I shall spoil you entirely, and Cousin Horace will feel like sending me home in disgrace, if he doesn't actually do it."

"No danger of that. I should be less surprised to hear him say he feared I should spoil you. But he told me to go to bed, and if I'm not there pretty soon, he may say I shall not go to the city tomorrow. And besides, I don't want to disobey my dear father, though he should not so much as say I'm not pleased with you."

"Then good night, dear, I'll run back to my room and get to bed, too, as fast as I can," Annis returned, giving Elsie a kiss and hurrying away.

The next day's shopping was a decided success, and the two little girls managed to get a great deal of enjoyment out of it. Mildred was not far behind them in that. She had seldom set herself a sweeter task than the selection and preparing of these gifts for the dear ones at home. For some, only the materials were bought and then fashioned into beautiful things by her own deft fingers, many a tender thought and many a loving prayer weaving themselves in among the stitches.

Annis and Elsie also made some pretty things and had them ready quickly, though Mr. Dinsmore would not allow any neglect of either lessons or outdoor exercise, and they as well as the ladies were occasionally hindered by calls.

Elsie had a number of little girl friends in the families which kept up a more or less intimate acquaintance at the Oaks and Roselands, who when their mothers or older sisters came to call upon Mrs. Landreth and Mrs. Dinsmore were allowed to come with them as callers upon Elsie and Annis.

It was no unusual thing for Mr. Dinsmore to take Elsie with him when making informal visits upon neighbors and friends, whether Rose accompanied him or not. And he made no objection to her going with her mamma and cousins to return those calls of her young friends, which they did as soon as the all-important box had been dispatched.

He and Dr. Landreth were usually of the party also, and the hospitable cordiality with which they were everywhere received made the little visits a pleasure for all.

The visit to Ion was the most enjoyable of any, as both Mrs. Travilla and her son were so very kind and knew so well how to please and entertain their guests, both older and younger. Mr. Travilla was fond of young girls, and Elsie was a very great favorite with both his mother and himself.

He had a good many pretty and interesting things to show to her and Annis, as well as to the older people: paintings, engravings, flowers, birds and other live pets, besides a cabinet of curiosities. Some of these last were relics of the Revolutionary War, and each had a story connected with it. He told one or two but said there was not time now for more, or to go into the details of any. That must all be deferred for the longer visit he and his mother hoped soon to have from them.

"We should like," he added, "to have you all here for a week or two, or as much longer as you please, but if the older people cannot afford us so much of their valuable time, we think we must at least have the little girls. What do you say to it, Dinsmore?"

Elsie turned eagerly to hear her father's reply. Annis listened anxiously for it, too, for both were greatly interested in everything connected with the Revolution and thought a week at Ion very desirable.

Mr. Dinsmore looked at them with an indulgent smile. "I see they would like to accept our kind invitation, Travilla," he said, "as doubtless we all should. Yet while thanking you and Mrs. Travilla for it, I think we must beg a little time to consider the matter. There must be a visit to Roselands, some entertaining at the Oaks, too, and it will not do to make pleasure the business of life, for it cannot be all holiday to any of us."

"That is very true," said Mrs. Travilla, "and those dear girls need to be garnering up knowledge now, in their youth, to make them ready for the duties and responsibilities of later years. Still, I hope, Horace, you will find that you can spare them to us for at least a few days. Their presence would brighten up the old place delightfully."

"You are very kind, my dear madam."

"To myself, yes. Edward and I are very fond of children, and your little daughter has always been an especial favorite with us both, as I am sure you know. If you should ever want to get rid of her," she added playfully, "we will be ready at a moment's notice to take her off your hands."

"Ah, yes, when?" he said, turning upon his child a look of unutterable love, joy, and fatherly pride.

CHAPTER XV

Sweet beauty sleeps upon thy brow,
And floats before my eyes;
As meek and pure as doves art thou,
Or beings of the skies.

—ROBERT MORRIS

"ELSIE, DON'T YOU want to spend that week at Ion? I think it would be just lovely! I'd a great deal rather go there for a long visit than to Roselands," Annis said, taking off her hat and twirling it about in her hands, though her thoughts were evidently not on it.

They had just driven home from Ion and were in Elsie's dressing room, Aunt Chloe busy about the person of her nursling.

"Yes, I should like to go very much indeed!" was the quick, earnest rejoinder.

"Then coax your father to let us."

Elsie shook her head. "That would be the surest way to make him say no. But you can go, Annis, if Cousin Mildred is willing, and I think it likely she will be. Don't you?"

"As if I'd care the least bit to go without you!" Annis exclaimed half indignantly. "But are you never allowed to coax?"

"No, not at all when papa is the person. He generally says yes or no at once, and then that's the end of it. Sometimes he says, 'I will consider the matter,' or 'I am not ready to decide that question yet,' and then I must just wait patiently till his answer is ready. I think mamma and Mr. Travilla can sometimes persuade him when they try, and I do hope they will try. You know," she added with a merry look, "he wouldn't be so rude to them as to refuse to listen to anything they might want to say."

"No, and I think he might be as polite to you."

"Papa always is polite to me, I think," Elsie answered gravely. "But you know, it's his duty to train me up right, so he has to make rules and see that I obey them."

"Oh, yes, of course! And I ought not to find the least fault with him, to you anyhow."

"Dar, darlin', I'se done wid fixin' you," remarked Aunt Chloe, smoothing down the folds of Elsie's dress. "Now, Miss Annis, what kin I do fo' you? I reckon de suppah bell ring fo' long."

Not long after supper, Mr. Dinsmore and Elsie were left sole occupants of the parlor. Dr. Landreth had gone to the library to do some writing, being much occupied just now with the business which had brought him South, the ladies were engaged with their babies, and Annis had run after Mildred as she left the room.

Mr. Dinsmore was pacing thoughtfully to and fro, Elsie seated beside the center table, turning pages in some new books but now and then stealing a furtive glance at her father, very much wishing he would call her to him, broach the subject of the invitation to Ion, and say that he intended to let her accept it.

Presently, she caught his eye, and pausing at her side, he laid his hand caressingly on her head. "What is it?" he asked, smiling down into the wistful, eager little face. "I see that my little girl has something to say to me. Come, sit on my knee and tell me all that is in your heart."

He took her hand as he spoke, led her to an easy chair, and seating himself therein drew her to his knee.

"Now, my darling, say on."

"Papa," she said, putting an arm around his neck and gazing straight into his eyes, with hers brimful of filial love to him and joy in his love for her, "don't you know all about it? You almost always know what I'm thinking about and what I want."

"Never mind how much I know. I choose to have you tell me," he said, softly touching his lips to the white forehead and the round, rosy cheek.

"Well then, father," she answered, dwelling slightly with an indescribably sweet and tender intonation upon that last word, "it is that Annis and I would like—oh, very much!—to accept the invitation to Ion, especially if you will go, too. I'm not quite sure I do wish to go without you."

"Well, daughter, I think you know that I dearly love to gratify you."

"Yes, papa, oh, yes indeed! And I'll try not to want to go if you don't think it best."

"That is my own dear child," he said, smiling fondly upon her. "I have been thinking that you and Annis might enjoy having a little company of your young friends here to spend a week or so of the holidays. What do you say to that?"

"Papa! What a nice idea!" she cried, clapping her hands.

"Your mamma and I will probably have some older guests visiting us at the same time. Mrs. and Mr. Travilla, I hope, among others. I trust they will enjoy it, and feel content with a shorter visit from us than they so kindly proposed, and that Annis and you will be satisfied also."

"I shall, papa, and I presume she will. But please tell me whom I may invite."

"You may first tell me whom you wish to ask. We will make out a list together," he said, taking a notebook and pencil from his pocket. "We have some weeks before us, but it may be as well to send out our invitations at once, lest we should be forestalled by someone else. Now then, what names have you to suggest?"

"Carrie Howard, Lucy Carrington, Isabel Carleton, Mary Leslie, Flora Arnott, and—papa, am I to ask anybody from Roselands?"

"No, I shall attend to that. We are all to dine there day after tomorrow, and I shall tell Enna she will be welcome to come and stay the week out, if she behaves nicely, but that I shall keep an eye on her and send her home if she shows her usual ill temper and disposition to domineer. Your mamma and I will invite your grandpa and his wife and your Aunt Adelaide. Louis and Lora will not, I presume, care to come—your party being too young and ours too old for them."

"But Walter, papa?"

"Yes, Walter must be invited. Edward and Herbert Carrington, too, and a few other well-behaved boys of suitable age. They will entertain each other and probably spend most of their time out of doors. These will be enough for you to invite to spend the week. We may, perhaps, have a larger party for Christmas Eve. You may if you wish."

"Dear father, how very kind and indulgent you are to me!" she said with loving gratitude. "I ought to be the best and most obedient of children."

"I think you are, my darling, and every day I thank God for giving me so dear, so precious a treasure as my only daughter. Suppose we go now to my study and write these invitations, if you are not too tired."

"Oh, I'm not tired at all, papa, and I think it would be nice to have it done because Annis and I are going to be very busy making Christmas things."

"And learning lessons," he added as he rose and led her from the room. "They must always be attended to first. You will no doubt find it difficult at times to concentrate your thoughts upon them, but you can do so if sufficiently determined, and I shall be strict in requiring it. It will be good mental discipline for you."

"Yes, sir," she responded with a half-sigh, as they entered the study hand in hand.

"Ah," he said playfully, bending down to look into her face, "papa does not seem to you quite so indulgent as you thought him a little while ago."

"Yes, papa, in everything you think for my

good. And indeed, I do often thank you in my heart for not indulging me in other things."

"I don't doubt it, my dear, submissive little daughter," he said in tenderest tones, imprinting a kiss on the sweet, ruby lips as she lifted her face to his.

"Now sit down here at your writing desk and let me see if you know how to word an invitation."

"But I don't, papa, so please dictate to me," she said, opening her desk and taking out a quantity of delicately tinted and perfumed notepaper and envelopes bearing her monogram.

"Very well."

"But if you would write them for me, papa, that would be better still. I'm afraid I don't write well enough."

"I think you write a very neat hand when you try," he said, dipping her pen into the ink and giving it to her.

"I shall try my very best now, papa," she answered. "I'll write Isabel Carleton's first, if you will please tell me how."

Half an hour later, she wiped and laid away the pen with a sigh of relief, then glanced with complacency at the little pile of dainty-looking notes on the table beside her desk.

"Thank you, papa, for your kind help," she said, turning to him.

"You are entirely welcome, my darling," he answered. "And I am well pleased with your part of the work; the writing is very neat and legible. I shall send a servant with them in the morning. Now let us go back to the parlor, for your mamma and cousins are probably there again. and I suppose you would like to tell Annis what you have been doing."

"Oh, yes, sir, and I think she'll be pleased."

They met Mrs. Dinsmore in the hall.

"Letters, Rose?" her husband said inquiringly as she came swiftly toward him.

"Notes of invitation, I think," she replied, pausing to look them over. "Yes, one for you and me," she said, handing it to him, "one for Dr. and Mrs. Landreth, one for Annis, and one for Elsie."

"For me, mamma!" cried the little girl, holding out an eager hand for it. "And Annis's. Mamma, may I take it to her?"

"Yes," Rose replied, giving her the two. "Do you know where she and her sister are?"

"Probably in the parlor," Mr. Dinsmore said, leading the way there.

They found the doctor, Mildred, and Annis all there and delivered them their notes.

"Papa, may I read mine?" Elsie asked softly, standing close at his side. "I haven't opened it yet."

"You may," he answered, with an approving smile.

"From the Howards of Pinegrove," said the doctor. "Well, we accept, I suppose, as a matter of course, as there seems to be nothing to prevent."

"Nothing for me, I believe," Mildred said, "except that I don't like to leave my baby long enough to attend an evening party."

"Nor I mine," said Rose.

"Oh, we'll make then an excuse for coming home early," said the doctor.

"Elsie, are you going?" Annis asked.

Elsie looked at her father with wistful, beseeching eyes.

"Cousin Horace, you will let her go, won't you?" Annis urged in her most persuasive tones.

"Are you very desirous to do so, daughter?" he asked, drawing Elsie to him, smoothing back the hair from her forehead with caressing hand, and gazing tenderly into the depths of the sweet, pleading eyes lifted to his.

"Oh, yes indeed, dear papa, if you are willing! And you know you will be there too, to take care of me."

"You are not very strong, and I rather fear the late hours for you. But if you can contrive to take a good long nap in the afternoon of that day, I will let you go, should nothing happen to prevent."

"Oh, thank you, papa!" she cried in transport of joy, putting her arms round his neck to hug and kiss him.

"Of course," he said, looking at Mildred, "I am taking it for granted that Annis is to go."

"It would hardly do to separate such fast friends," Mildred said, smiling upon her little sister's eager, entreating face, "and I am sure I may safely let Annis go wherever Elsie goes with her father's approval."

"And I never go anywhere without it, Cousin Milly, and never expect to as long as I live," Elsie said, with a sweet, happy little laugh as she gave her father another affectionate hug.

Then she whispered in his ear, "Wasn't it odd that Carrie Howard should invite me just when I was inviting her? May I tell Annis now? May everybody hear what we've been doing?"

He nodded a smiling assent, and she immediately availed herself of the permission.

The older people all entered into her pleasure, and Annis was greatly pleased with her news.

CHAPTER XVI

Costly thy habit as thy purse can buy,
But not expressed in fancy; rich, not gaudy;
For the apparel oft proclaims the man.

—SHAKESPEARE

"MILLY," ANNIS SAID, following her sister, as usual, when she retired for the night to her own apartments, "what shall I wear to the party? Have I anything suitable?"

"I'm afraid not, dear, but you shall have a new dress and as pretty a one as can be found. We have ten days for the buying and making."

"But there won't be time to ask father or mother if I may have it."

"And no need," Mildred said merrily. "I am rich now, you know, and it will be a dear delight to me to deck my little sister for the party."

"Oh, thank you, Milly, you're just the best and kindest sister in the world!" exclaimed the little girl, dancing about in delight, then stopping short to throw her arms about Mildred and give her a vigorous hug and kiss.

Mildred returned the embrace, saying with a quiet smile, "You forget that I am pleasing myself. And don't you think that Zillah, Ada, or

147

Fan would do as much for you under the same circumstances?"

"Yes, and I think I should for them. I think we all love one another very much, and ah, but I do want to hear how they like their presents!"

"They won't get them for some weeks yet, you must remember, and then their letters of acknowledgement will take some time to reach us."

"Milly, what sort of dress shall it be?" Annis asked, returning to the original topic of discourse.

"Something white I think, but we can decide better upon the material when we see what they have in the stores."

"I hope Elsie will wear white, too. I think it will prettier for us both."

"I daresay she will. Her father likes to see her in white, and, of course, he will say what she is to wear."

"Yes, and she has so many lovely white dresses. I'm sure she'll grow too large for them before they're half worn out."

"Yes, no doubt," Mildred said with a slight smile. "But now, dear, isn't it time to say good night?"

"Yes, when I've had a peep at darling wee Percy," Annis returned, stealing softly to the side of the crib and bending over the little sleeper with a face all aglow with loving admiration. "Oh, Milly, he's so sweet and pretty!" she whispered, turning to the young mother who stood close at her side. "I'd like so much to kiss him, but I won't, for fear of waking him—the precious child."

On going down, Annis found Elsie in her

dressing room being made ready for bed. "May I stay and talk a little?" she asked.

"Yes, while mammy is undressing me," Elsie said. "I do want to have a long talk, but papa's orders are to get to bed and to sleep as fast as I can and leave the talking for tomorrow."

"Then we must, of course. But I want to tell you that Milly is going to get me a new dress for the party—a white one she thinks. Isn't she good? And won't you wear white, too?"

"I don't know. I hadn't thought about it yet, and papa hasn't said anything, either."

"Well, you have such quantities of beautiful dresses that you don't need to think till you're just going to put it on."

"I don't need to think at all," Elsie returned with a happy little laugh. "I have only to ask papa what he will choose to have me wear, and sometimes he saves me even that trouble by telling me unasked."

"I don't know whether I'd quite prefer that or not," Annis said. "But good night, I'll go now, for I see you are ready for bed."

Annis fell asleep that night and woke again next morning full of pleasing anticipation of the coming festivities. But she wisely determined to give her whole mind to her lessons until after recitation.

Her preparations were almost finished when Elsie came in, her eyes shining and her face full of some pleasurable excitement. She had been up for more than an hour and had had her morning Bible reading with her father and a little chat afterward.

"Good morning, Annis," she said. "Make haste and come with me. I've something to show you!"

"Have you? Well, I'm ready now."

Elsie led the way to a part of the house Annis had never seen, bringing her at length into a large room where two 0women were busily at work, one sewing by hand, the other on a machine. Both faces brightened noticeably at sight of their little mistress.

"Good morning, Aunt Kitty," she said in her sweet, gentle tones, addressing the older woman, who hastily laid down her sewing to hand a chair for each little lady. "I've brought my cousin to see you and some of the pretty things kept here."

"Is you, honey? Well, you knows I'se always pow'rful glad to see yo' lubly face in hyar. An' what's yo' cousin's name, Miss Elsie?"

"Annis Keith, Aunt Kitty. Rachel," she said, turning to the younger servant, "how are you today? Is that bad cold quite gone?"

"Yes, tank you, Miss Elsie, an' I'se pretty well, exceptin' a misery in de back."

"I think mamma would say you shouldn't work on the machine today if your back hurts you," remarked Elsie with a compassionate look.

"Oh, chile, 'tain't nothin'!" exclaimed Aunt Kitty with a contemptuous sniff directed at her companion. "Rachel, she's always 'plainin' ob a misery somewheres, and de mo' you nuss her up and let her off from work, de wuss it grows. She better work away and forgit it. Dat's how dis chile does."

Elsie seemed too eager about something else to pay attention to the remark. She had taken a key from her pocket, and unlocking a large wardrobe on the farther side of the room, she said, "Annis, won't you come here for a moment?"

Annis was beside her instantly.

"Don't you think this is pretty?" Elsie asked, showing her some beautifully fine India mull.

"Oh, lovely!" Annis exclaimed. "Are you going to have a dress made of that?"

"Yes, to wear to Carrie's party, and I want you to have one, so that we will be dressed alike. Papa bought it some time ago, a whole piece, I think he said, and I shall take it as a great favor," she added in an undertone and with a very winning, persuasive look into Annis's eyes, "if you will accept a dress of it as a present from me."

"Thank you ever so much, but—I'm afraid I oughtn't," Annis said, hesitating, blushing, and looking half pleased, half as if the offer were slightly wounding to her pride of independence.

"Why not?" Elsie asked entreatingly. "Papa wants you to—it was he who thought of it first— and I shall be so sorry if you refuse. I've quite set my heart on having our dresses exactly alike, just as if you were my sister. You know I've never had a sister, and I've always wanted one so much."

"You are just as kind as you can be, Elsie," Annis returned, putting her arms round her cousin and kissing her affectionately. "But I don't think Mildred would want me to take it. Anyhow, I must ask her first. Couldn't she buy me one just like it in the city?"

"I don't know. Mamma and papa both said when he bought this that it was an uncommonly beautiful piece."

"Oh, it is beautiful, Elsie, so beautiful that I don't like to have you give it to me—it must have cost so much!"

"That makes it all the more suitable for you, dear Annis. And it is not at all generous of me to offer it, because it does not cost me the least self-denial to part with it. Won't you take it?"

Annis hesitated for a moment, then said with frank cordiality, "Yes, I will, if Milly doesn't object. You know she's in mother's place to me while I am here."

"Thank you!" Elsie said delightedly. "I do so want you to have it. Let us run and ask Cousin Mildred now. No, on second thought, I do believe it will be best to consult papa first. He always knows just what it is best to do. But wait, I want to show you the trimming for our dresses. They must be trimmed alike too, papa says."

She lifted the lid of a box and drew out the end of a piece of lace so fine, soft, rich, and beautiful in design that even Annis, though not a connoisseur of the article, could not fail to perceive that it must be very costly.

She exclaimed at its beauty, adding, "You could never think of giving any of that away, Elsie! Cousin Horace could not have meant that!"

"But indeed he did," Elsie answered happily. "He doesn't consider anything too good for you, nor do I. But there's the breakfast bell, and we must hurry down."

They found Mr. Dinsmore alone in the breakfast room. He greeted them with a smile and, taking Annis's hand, gave her a good-morning kiss.

"Now it's my turn, papa," Elsie said in a merry tone, holding up a face so bright, loving, and winsome that it would have taken a very cold and unresponsive nature to refuse her invitation.

Her father did not, though he said laughingly as he bestowed the caress, "As if you had not had half a dozen more or less already this morning! Well, what success?" he asked with a kindly glance at Annis.

"Oh, I had to coax her, papa, but she will if Cousin Milly will."

"Ah, is that it? Well, leave Mildred to me."

"No, sir," exclaimed Dr. Landreth's voice from behind him, "it can't be done! Mildred belongs to me."

"Ah, good morning to you both!" said Mr. Dinsmore, turning at the sound to find the doctor and his wife both there. "I've no idea of interfering with your claims, sir. One wife's enough for me to manage," he said with a merry glance at Rose, who entered at that moment by another door.

"A trifle too much sometimes, if the truth were told, isn't she?" Rose retorted as she took her place at the head of the table, the others seating themselves at the same time.

"My dear, you should never tell tales out of school," said Mr. Dinsmore.

There was a general laugh, then a moment's pause for all to recover their gravity, and he asked a blessing on the food.

At the first opportunity, Mildred remarked, "You have roused my curiosity, Cousin Horace, and I think are bound to gratify it. In regard to what am I to be left to you?"

"Didn't I put my veto on that?" queried her husband.

"Yes, and yet I venture to assert that you are every whit as curious as I know what it all meant. Cousin Horace, you are called upon to explain."

"Will you do me a favor?"

"Gladly, if it is in my power."

"There, children, you see it's all settled with a word."

"What's settled?" asked Mildred.

"That Annis shall have, or rather already has, your consent to her acceptance of a little present from Elsie. I shall explain further later."

After breakfast and prayers, Mildred was taken to the sewing room and shown the intended gift while the desired explanation was made.

She was not so proud in her wealth as she had been in her poverty, and thus she gracefully accepted for Annis, though she perceived that the present was by no means the trifle Mr. Dinsmore had represented it.

"I had intended to give Annis her dress," she said, "but I doubt if I could find anywhere such exquisitely fine mull or lace so beautiful and costly as this. And I think it will be very nice to have the dressed alike. This lace is superb!" she said, examining it more closely. "You are making Annis a most generous gift, Cousin Horace," she added, looking up with cordial affection into his handsome, kindly face as he stood by her side, "and I thank you and dear Elsie, a thousand times."

"Not at all. I feel myself the obliged party," he returned, "and I want you to do us the further favor of allowing Annis's dress to be made up here. Aunt Kitty and Rachel are accomplished seamstresses and dressmakers and will be well pleased to have the job."

"Dat we will, Massa," responded Aunt Kitty, as he turned to her as if for confirmation of what he had said, "an' I spects we kin do de work up 'bout right."

This offer also Mildred accepted with thanks, remarking merrily, "You never do anything by halves, Cousin Horace."

The little girls, greatly pleased at the result of the conference, ran off in high glee to take their accustomed outdoor exercise, then settled themselves to their lessons with a determined will to think of nothing else until they were learned.

So fully occupied were they with the business at hand that they were not aware of the departure of their elders on a shopping expedition to the city. When they felt themselves fully prepared with their tasks, they put aside their books, rather wondering that Mr. Dinsmore was so much later than usual in coming to hear their recitations. But they practiced some duets they were learning together on the piano, and the time did not seem long till the carriage drove up and their four elders walked in upon them looking as if they brought a pleasant surprise, as indeed they did. Mr. Dinsmore and Rose each put a small paper parcel into Elsie's hand, Dr. Landreth and Mildred doing the same by Annis.

With eager fingers the children made haste to undo the packages and bring their contents to light, the givers looking on with faces full of pleased anticipation.

Elsie's presents proved to be two very elegant sashes—a pale blue and a rich cream-white. Mildred's present to Annis was the same: two sashes exactly matching her cousin's, the doctor's a jewel box, which being opened showed a dainty lining of pale blue satin, on which reposed an exquisitely beautiful necklace and bracelets of pearls scarcely inferior in size and value to those belonging to Elsie, which Annis had so often admired, never dreaming that such would ever fall to her lot.

She went into a transport of delight and hugged and kissed not Mildred only but her new brother to his heart's content.

Elsie fully sympathized with Annis's pleasure and was quietly happy with her own gifts and grateful to her kind parents.

CHAPTER XVII

Patience, my lord! why, 'tis the soul of peace;
Of all the virtues 'tis the nearest kin to heaven.

— DECKER

WHEN ALONE WITH Annis that evening, Mildred said to her, "I had a talk with Uncle Dinsmore today. You know we are all engaged to dine at Roselands tomorrow, and he wants us— that is, my husband, you, and me—to go prepared to stay at least a week."

"Oh, Milly, I don't want to! cried Annis. "Do you think I must? I wish we didn't have to go!"

"It is pleasanter here, especially so to you, I suppose, but consider, dear, how very kind Uncle Dinsmore has always been to us and how rude and ungrateful it would seem to decline his invitation."

"I'm willing to go for tomorrow, but what is to be done about my lessons if I stay a whole week?"

"I spoke of that, and uncle said you should be brought over every day for the lesson hours and taken back again. Won't that do, little lady? Mildred asked with playfully affectionate look and tone.

"Yes," Annis said, her face brightening a little. "I don't want to be, or to seem ungrateful to anybody, and I think I can stand it in that way for a week. And I'll try to like the cousins there, though I'm sure they're not half so nice as these here."

"No," assented Mildred, "but you might travel the world over without finding another such little girl as Elsie."

"Yes indeed, sister! I grow fonder of her every day. She's so sweet and bright, often merry and full of innocent fun, without a particle of rudeness, so gentle and humble and unselfish. She doesn't think herself good at all, but I think she's as nearly perfect as anybody can be in this world."

"And I quite agree with you," said Mildred. "No wonder her father dotes on her as he does."

"And she on him. But the way Enna sometimes treats her makes me angry. I can hardly help telling Miss Enna she ought to be ashamed of herself, and could almost scold Elsie for being so meek and patient."

"Meekness and patience are very good things, little sister," Mildred said with a slight smile. "I often wish I had more of them."

"You needn't then. You have quite enough, I think," returned Annis.

"The Bible bids us 'let patience have her perfect work,' and it is certainly a lack of the spirit of forgiveness that makes us irritable and impatient under little annoyances, slights, and rudenesses," remarked Mildred. Opening her Bible to the seventh chapter of Ecclesiastes, she read aloud, "And the patient in spirit is better than the proud in spirit."

"But, Milly, do you think it means we ought to

put up with everything and just let people trample on us?"

"No, I agree with Edmund Burke that 'there is a limit at which forbearance ceases to be a virtue.' See here, Solomon says, 'Surely oppression maketh a wise man mad.' And," she said, turning to the New Testament, "here in Acts we read that when the keeper of the prison said to Paul, 'The magistrates have sent to let you go, now therefore depart and go in peace,' Paul's answer was, 'They have beaten us openly uncondemned, being Romans, and have cast us into prison, and now do they thrust us out privily? nay verily, but let them come themselves and fetch us out.'"

"Yes," said Annis meditatively, as if thinking aloud, "I've an idea he wouldn't have put up with as much as Elsie does from Enna."

"What is it Enna does that seems to you so unendurable?" asked Mildred with some curiosity.

"Oh, it isn't so much what she does, or even says, as it is her sneering, contemptuous tone and manner, as if Elsie were ever so much younger and sillier than herself, when she is really older and a great deal wiser. I spoke to Elsie about it one day, and she said she was very glad Enna didn't go any farther, because her papa had ordered her to tell him if Enna abused her, and, of course, she must obey, and she did dislike so very much to do it."

Elsie seldom found much enjoyment in a visit to Roselands. Her Aunt Adelaide was the only member of the family there between whom and herself there was a strong mutual attachment, though Lora and Walter were not unkind and sometimes treated her even quite affectionately.

She and Annis were not in haste to be off from the Oaks on the day of the dinner party, so they did not ask to be excused from lessons in order to accompany Rose and Mildred in the family carriage. They had their morning walk together, Annis took her riding lesson, then the usual time was spent in study and recitation.

After that they made their dinner preparations, and Elsie drove Annis over in her own little phaeton, her father riding by its side all the way to Roselands.

It was not strictly a family party. There were several gentlemen guests beside Mr. Dinsmore and Dr. Landreth, among whom the children were glad to see Mr. Travilla. His mother was there also and not too busy talking to the grown-up people to find time for a little chat with her two young favorites.

They had each brought a bit of fancy work, and until dinner was announced, they sat in the drawing room, busy and demurely quiet, listening with interest to the talk that was going on around them, but taking no part in it unless a question or remark were addressed particularly to them.

The moment Walter and Enna caught sight of the phaeton driving up the avenue, they ran out to the veranda, and hardly waiting to greet their brother and the little girls, asked eagerly to be allowed to take a drive in it.

"It belongs to Elsie," Mr. Dinsmore answered.

"Papa," she said in an undertone, as he helped

her out, "I am willing if you are. But please tell them they are not to ill use the ponies in any way."

"I shall ride alongside and see that they do not," he said. "You and Annis go in and say that I will be here in time for dinner."

"Say, Horace, say, can I drive?" Walter was repeating impatiently.

"Yes, Elsie says you may."

"Then I'm going too," cried Enna, stepping in.

"No, Enna, you cannot go bareheaded and with nothing round you, and there's not time to wait for you to fix. And I'll not have you, because you'll do nothing but scold and quarrel all the way."

"No, she won't, for I shall be close at hand to keep her in order," said Mr. Dinsmore, remounting his horse.

"And here comes Fanny with a hood and shawl for me," said Enna as a servant-maid came hurrying out with the articles mentioned.

Walter, like the gentlemanly little fellow he was when not provoked beyond endurance by Enna's temper and wilfulness, helped the girl to wrap the shawl about his sister's shoulders. The hood was tied on, and they were off. Down the avenue and out into the road they went, the ponies at a brisk trot, Mr. Dinsmore's horse side-by-side with the phaeton.

"What a splendid little turnout it is!" exclaimed Walter. "Wish I had one like it."

"You have a good pony," said his brother, "and I should think would, at least as a general thing, prefer riding to driving."

"Horace, mayn't I drive?" asked Enna in a whining tone.

"Perhaps Walter will resign the reins to you for part of the way," Mr. Dinsmore answered, "but we have not time to go very far."

"You may drive to the end of the next field," Walter said, giving her the reins.

"Such a little bit of a way!" she grumbled, and Enna would certainly have held on to them when the designated spot was reached if Mr. Dinsmore had not been so close at hand.

He seemed in a most amiable mood, conversing with the two children in an affable and entertaining manner, but Enna knew he could be very stern and authoritative on occasion. So a pout was the only evidence of displeasure she ventured upon when Walter resumed the reins.

But no notice was taken of it by either brother, and presently Mr. Dinsmore began talking of the expected festivities at the Oaks and gave them their invitation, adding, "You, Enna, will be very welcome to come and stay the whole week if you can enjoy yourself and let others do the same."

"What do you mean by that?" she asked snappishly.

"That you must be pleasant-tempered and not domineering over your little mates but willing to yield your wishes to theirs to a reasonable extent. In a word, be polite and unselfish."

"I shan't go!"

"Very well, please yourself in that."

"I'll go, Horace, thank you," Walter said. "I wouldn't miss it for a good deal."

"I say it's too bad," Enna burst out, "that people are always calling me selfish and ill-natured and domineering. I should think I've as good a right to have my way as anybody else."

"Not all the time," said Mr. Dinsmore. "And hardly at all when you are a minority of one against a majority of half a dozen or more. But I certainly did not say you were selfish and domineering."

On their return, they found themselves barely in time for dinner. The party not being very large, the children were allowed to dine with the older people, and Elsie, to her no small content, was seated between her father and Mr. Travilla, Annis being on the latter gentleman's other side.

Both little girls were well waited upon and were quietly happy and contented, saying next to nothing themselves but enjoying the conversation of their elders.

Walter, seated on the opposite side of the table, seemed in excellent spirits.

"That's a splendid little turnout of yours," he said, looking across at Elsie, "I tell you, I enjoyed the drive, only it wasn't half long enough. But you'll lend it to me again, won't you?"

She smiled and nodded assent.

"I'm going to the Oaks to spend Christmas week, but Enna says she isn't," he went on in a lowered voice, glancing in Enna's direction.

Elsie's eyes followed his, and she saw that Enna's face was clouded and angry. She was sorry but made no remark about it.

After dinner, Lora invited Elsie and Annis to her room to show them some pretty things she was making as Christmas gifts for her father and mother and to talk about what she should wear to the party at Pine Grove. She was quite surprised to hear that they were both invited, still more that Elsie's father had consented to let her go. Then she wanted to know just how they were to be dressed.

Enna came in while they were on that subject and exclaimed angrily that it was too bad they should be invited and she not.

"You are too young," said Lora, "and besides, always contrive to make yourself disagreeable wherever you go."

Lora's words were by no means as oil upon the troubled waters. Enna flew into a violent passion and abused her sister and niece in turn. Lora was "a mean, spiteful, hateful thing, Elsie not a bit better."

"Why, Enna, what have I done?" Elsie asked in surprise but with a gentle patience and forbearance that ought to have disarmed her accuser.

"You've done a great deal," stormed Enna. "I believe you're always running to Horace with tales about me. And you've gone and got ahead of me by inviting all the girls to the Oaks for Christmas, so that I can't have any of them here."

"Now, Enna," expostulated Lora, "there's no use in talking so. You know mamma has said she wouldn't be bothered with a houseful of company this Christmas, and we younger ones are all going away to spend the holidays."

"No, I'm not," interrupted the irate Enna. "I'd rather a thousand times stay at home than go to the old Oaks, to have Horace lecturing and reproving and Elsie running to him all the time with tales about me."

"Oh, Enna!" Elsie exclaimed, blushing painfully. "I never tell anything about you unless papa orders me, and then you know I can't help it."

"You could if you chose. I'd never tell tales for being ordered!" returned Enna with scornful look and tone.

"No," remarked Lora, coolly, "but you are ready enough to do it without. And you needn't say another word about Elsie getting ahead of you in sending out invitations, for you never thought of doing so till you heard that she had. And besides, you are so unpopular with your mates that they would find some excuse for not coming, if you did invite them."

Elsie was not sorry that at that moment a summons came for her from her father.

She obeyed at once, Annis and Lora accompanying her to the drawing room, where they found she was wanted to play and sing, some of the stranger guests having expressed a desire to hear her.

It was always a trial to her to play before strangers, but she sat down at the piano, in obedience to her father's direction, without hesitation or excuse, and acquitted herself to his complete satisfaction and apparently to that of all the guests.

She did not leave the drawing room again or have any more talk with Enna, until it was time to prepare for the ride home.

It seemed lonely to go back without the cousins and especially to leave Annis behind. But as compensation, she had her father and mother all to herself for the whole evening and was allowed to sit longer than usual in her favorite seat upon his knee.

Annis was there again the next morning in time to prepare her lessons for the day, and the two met as joyfully as if the separation had been for weeks.

After their recitations, Annis had to have her new dress fitted and then take her riding lesson before returning to Roselands.

Elsie saw her off, then went to her papa's study, where he was busily writing. She knew she was welcome there if she did nothing to disturb him, so she took a book and seated herself on the farther side of the room.

Mr. Dinsmore was still at his writing desk when a servant came in with a visiting card which he handed to his master, saying he had shown the gentleman into the parlor.

"It is a business call," Mr. Dinsmore said, glancing at the card. "Just show him in here, John."

Elsie had become so deeply interested in her book that she heard nothing of this, nor was she aware of the entrance of the caller, who was courteously received by Mr. Dinsmore and invited to take a chair which John set for him near to that of his master.

The two then fell into earnest talk, and presently something said by the stranger caught Elsie's ear. She withdrew her attention from the book and fixed it upon him and the subject of his discourse.

He was pleading the cause of Home Missions, telling of the needs, the labors, trials, and privations of those who were carrying the gospel to the destitute regions of our own land, especially the far West and Northwest. Money was needed for the support of the laborers now in the field and for others ready to go as soon as the necessary means should be provided.

Elsie laid aside her book and softly drew near her father's chair. He had forgotten her presence and did not notice her approach, for he too was deeply interested in what the stranger was saying, and when he seemed to have concluded, responded at once with a liberal contribution to the cause.

As he handed the gentleman his check, a little voice at his side said softly, "Papa, may I give something, too?"

"Ah, daughter, is it you? I had forgotten that you were here," he said, turning to her with a pleased smile. "Yes, you may, if you wish," he said, and he laid a blank check before her and put a pen in her hand.

"How much, papa?"

"I shall leave that to your decision."

She considered a moment, filled up the check, signed, and gave it to him. It was drawn for five hundred dollars.

Her look as her eyes met his was a little doubtful and timid. But he said, "Very well," smiling upon her and stroking her hair caressingly as he spoke. Then, turning to the stranger, he introduced her. "This, sir, is my little daughter, and she wishes to make a contribution of her own to this good cause."

The gentleman shook hands with her, regarding the sweet child face with evident admiration and saying a few pleasant words, then glancing at the check she had given him, uttered an exclamation of gratified surprise.

"She is well able to give it and has my full consent," Mr. Dinsmore remarked in explanation, as the gentleman turned upon him an inquiring, half-hesitating look. As the latter rose to go, Mr. Dinsmore hospitably urged him to stay for dinner and until the next day, if he could.

He accepted the invitation to dine, thus giving them the opportunity to learn still more of the cause represented, but he took leave very soon after the conclusion of the meal.

CHAPTER XVIII

Humility, that low, sweet root,
From which all heavenly virtues shoot.

—MOORE

THE WEEK OF their partial separation passed more rapidly than Elsie and Annis had thought possible, yet they were very glad when it was over and they were again almost constantly together.

When lessons were done on the morning that Annis came back to stay, Elsie carried her off to the sewing room, saying their party dresses were finished and Aunt Kitty wanted to see them tried on to make sure that no alteration was needed.

Both were found to fit perfectly, and they were very neatly made and very beautiful and becoming.

"Oh, aren't they just too lovely for anything!" cried Annis, gazing at Elsie, then turning to survey her own graceful little figure in the glass.

"You look so sweet in yours, Annis," Elsie said, her eyes full of genuine, loving admiration as they went from the dress up to the bright, happy face of the wearer. "Let us run and show ourselves to mamma and Cousin Mildred. I think they are in mamma's boudoir."

The ladies were found, and their verdict was entirely satisfactory: they could see no room for improvement in the dresses.

"Or the faces either," Rose said in a whispered aside to Mildred.

"Both are very sweet and winsome, but Elsie's far the more beautiful of the two," Mildred returned in the same low tone but with a loving look at her little sister.

Then the gentlemen came in, and they, too, admired and commended.

"Now, little girls," Mr. Dinsmore said, "your ponies and my horse are standing ready, saddled and bridled at the door, and if you will exchange this finery for your riding habits, we will take a gallop. Annis is equal to that now, I think."

"Oh, thank you, Cousin Horace!" she exclaimed in delight. As they ran merrily to do his bidding, she said to Elsie, "We'll doff our finery willingly enough for that, won't we?"

"Yes, indeed we will! I'm so glad you enjoy riding, Annis. I always did, especially with papa for my escort.

They had their ride and enjoyed it greatly, too. Then there was an hour for needle work or anything they chose to do before dinner.

In the afternoon, they were starting out for a walk together about the grounds. Annis, who was a little in advance of Elsie, called back to her from the veranda, "The sun has gone under a cloud. Do you think there's any danger of rain before we get back?"

"I guess not," Elsie answered.

Her papa's study door was ajar, and she was quite near it as she spoke.

"Elsie!" came his voice in grave, reproving tones from within.

"Sir!" she said, hastening to him.

He was writing and for a moment seemed oblivious to her presence.

"I am here, papa," she said softly as he paused to dip his pen in the ink.

"I am not pleased with you," he remarked without looking at her.

"Oh, papa! Why?" The sweet voice was tremulous with pain and surprise.

"I cannot be pleased with you when you are not careful to obey me."

"Papa, I have intended to be so. I — I don't know what I have done that — that you bade me not."

"Think a moment. What was it you said as you passed the door just now?"

"Only three words, papa, in answer to Annis, 'I guess not.'"

"Ah! And what did I say to you the other day about using 'guess' in that way?"

"You forbade me," she faltered, her eyes filling with tears. "Oh, papa, please forgive me this once! I'll try never to forget again. I'm sorry, very sorry, dear papa."

He laid down his pen, turned toward her, and held out his arms.

She sprang into them, put hers about his neck, and laid her cheek to his.

"This once," he said, caressing her softly. "But my little girl must be careful not to forget again."

"You'd have to punish me another time?"

"Yes."

"I — I think —"

"Well?"

"I'm afraid I ought to be punished this time to help me to remember. But oh, please don't say I can't go to the party!"

"No, I shall not do that. It shall be free forgiveness this time. I think you are sorry enough to remember in future. Doubtless you think your papa is very strict and particular about your mode of expressing yourself, but someday you will thank me for it. Now go for your walk. We have kept Annis waiting quite long enough."

"Thank you, dear papa," she said, holding up her face for another kiss, "I think you are very, very kind!"

"Why, what kept you so long?" asked Annis as Elsie joined her on the veranda. "I though you were all ready and right behind me."

"Papa called me into his study; he had something to say to me," Elsie answered with a blush, turning away her face so that Annis might not see it and the tears in her eyes. "I'm sorry to have kept you waiting, cousin," she added in her own sweet, gentle tones.

"Never mind. It doesn't matter, and I didn't mean to complain," Annis said with cheerful good humor. "Oh, there's Mr. Travilla!" she exclaimed as a horseman was seen coming up the drive. "Let's wait and speak to him."

They stood still looking toward him, and in a moment he had dismounted close beside them and was shaking hands and asking if they and all the family were well.

"I'll put yo' hoss in de stable, Massa Travilla," said a servant, coming up and taking the bridle from his hand.

"Yes, if you please, Dick. I may perhaps stay some little time."

"Oh, yes, sir, you must stay to tea!" Elsie said. "You have not been here for several days, and we cannot let you leave us after a call only."

"Thank you, my dear," he returned with a pleased look. "You are setting out for a walk? I wish you would invite me to go with you."

"Oh, we should be glad, very glad, to have you!" both answered in a breath.

So he went with them and made himself very entertaining, telling them several amusing anecdotes and giving them various items of useful information.

When they returned to the house, Mr. Dinsmore met them on the veranda, shook hands with his friend, and stood talking with him for several minutes.

While her father was thus engaged Elsie drew quietly near his side, and taking unobserved possession of his hand, carried it to her lips.

He paused an instant in his talk, bent down, and kissed her, looking with tender, loving eyes into hers, which were half filled with repentant tears. "My darling!" he said softly, then straightening himself went on with what he had been saying but kept her hand in a close, loving clasp.

"You will, of course, stay and take supper with

us, Travilla?" he said, leading the way into the house, still with Elsie's hand in his.

"And, oh, Mr. Travilla!" exclaimed Annis, "Don't you want to see our party dresses? They're finished and are just the loveliest things that ever you saw!"

"Yes," he said, "I am much interested in the appearance you ladies are to make at the party."

So he was taken directly to Elsie's dressing room, where the dresses were exhibited to his admiring eyes.

Mr. Travilla stayed until very nearly Elsie's bedtime, and Mildred and the others lingered a little after he was gone, so that the little girl began to fear she would miss the usual private bit of chat with her father. She was particularly anxious for it tonight, for her tender little heart was still sore at thought of his words, "I am not pleased with you."

But at last she was left alone with him, even Rose having disappeared from the room in response to a call from the nursery.

The instant the door closed on the last of them, Mr. Dinsmore turned to his child with outstretched hand and a kind, fatherly smile, saying, "Come, daughter dear, we have not many minutes left before it will be time for you to go to bed."

"Papa, oh, papa!" she said, hastening to him and hiding her face on his breast. "Are you quite, quite please with me now?"

"Yes, darling, your fault is entirely forgiven, and now let it be forgotten. I think it will not be repeated, and I am glad to be able to say it is a rare thing for my little girl to be guilty of the slightest act of disobedience. You haven't told me about your afternoon's walk. Was it pleasant?"

"Oh, very nice!" she replied, lifting her head to wipe away her tears, and give him a grateful, loving look. "Mr. Travilla was with us and told us such nice stories. He is almost as entertaining and instructive in conversation as you yourself, papa."

"Almost!" he said, laughing. "Well, I can swallow the flattery because of the large admixture of filial love in it."

"Is it flattery when we are perfectly sincere, papa?" she asked.

"Not gross flattery," he said, "not meant as such at all in this case, I am sure. Love makes my little girl see her father through rose-colored glasses."

"But don't you like it?" she asked naïvely.

"Yes, I must confess I do," he returned with a look of amusement.

Annis was with Mildred, talking about the coming party. It would be quite an event in the child's life, and though very unwilling to miss it, she felt some shrinking and timidity at the prospect of meeting so many strange people in a strange place.

"I'm afraid I won't behave right, Milly," she said a little anxiously. "I wish you could tell me just how."

"Forget yourself, dear, and think only how to add to the enjoyment of others. Be modest and retiring—though I need hardly tell you that—but don't be troubled with the idea that people are watching you. They will have something else to attend to, and a little girl like you is not likely to be noticed in so large a company."

"That's nice!" Annis remarked with satisfaction. "I think it will be fun to watch the doings of the grown-up folks and listen to their talk without anybody taking notice of it—it will be almost as good as being invisible."

"Ah, don't be too sure of a great deal of fun to be gained in that way. Some of the talk at such gatherings is apt to be too insipid to be worth hearing, if nothing worse."

"Milly, I don't believe you care much for parties," Annis said, half in wonder and surprise and half inquiringly.

"No. I did once, but I got my fill of them long ago. Quiet home pleasures with those I love and who love me are now far more to my taste. Still, we owe something to neighbors and friends outside of our family, and one must not give up society altogether."

"You've made me feel more comfortable about going," remarked Annis.

"Why, I thought you were quite desirous to go, quite pleased with the prospect!" Mildred returned in surprise.

"Yes, I did want to go, and yet I felt frightened at the thought of seeing so many grand ladies and gentlemen all together. I was afraid I shouldn't behave right at all. It's very comfortable to think I can look at them and hardly be seen myself."

"You would not like to think your dress would miss being seen?" Mildred said playfully.

"No, indeed! It is so pretty."

"I wish mother could see you in it!"

"Yes, and you in yours, Milly," she said, glancing at a beautiful evening dress that had just come from the mantuamaker's. "I wonder what they are doing at home!"

"Probably getting ready for bed — Fan at least. I think she would not envy you your dress if it must be worn by its possessor to a large party."

"No, she's so bashful. Poor, dear Fan!"

"Now, daughter," Mr. Dinsmore said as they left the dinner table on the all-important day, "I want you to go and lie down. Sleep all afternoon if you can. And I should advise Annis to do the same."

Elsie obeyed, of course, Annis followed his advice, and both felt very fresh and bright when the time came for them to be arrayed for the party.

Aunt Chloe undertook the dressing of both, "so dat Miss Mildred needn't hab no botheration 'bout it," and she found no difficulty in accomplishing her task to the satisfaction of all concerned.

The two were dressed exactly alike except that Elsie wore a white sash and Annis a blue one.

When the last finishing touch had been given, they went into the library to show themselves to Mr. Dinsmore.

"Are you satisfied with us, papa?" Elsie asked as they presented themselves before him.

"Perfectly," he said, glancing from one to the other with a pleased smile, then bestowing a kiss upon each. "I hope you may enjoy yourselves very much indeed."

"Thank you, sir! Now I'm going up to Mildred," Annis said, running happily from the room.

Elsie looked wistfully at her father. "You are all ready, papa, aren't you?"

"Yes," he said, drawing her to his knee, "and as it will be far past your usual bedtime when we come home tonight, we must have our good time together now. Did you take you nap?"

"Oh, yes, sir. Mammy says I slept more than two hours."

"That is well. I could hardly have consented to let you go otherwise, because you are not strong enough to bear much loss of sleep. It is quite possible I may not be near you in the refreshment room at Pinegrove, so I tell you now that you are not to eat any rich cake or preserves or any salad."

Elsie laughed. "Why, papa," she said, giving him a hug, "you never let me eat such things at any time!"

"No, that is true, and yet I thought it as well to remind you lest you should be tempted to yield to hospitable urgency."

"Papa, I would not dis—" But a sudden recollection made her pause and drop her eyes, while a crimson tide swept over the fair face and neck.

"I have not a doubt that my dear little girl fully intends to be perfectly obedient," he said kindly, lifting the sweet, downcast face and pressing a kiss upon the ruby lips.

At that instant the door opened, and Rose entered in full evening dress.

"Will I do, my dear?" she asked. "Does your wife's attire meet your approval?"

"I am altogether satisfied with both it and her," was the gallant rejoinder. "Are the others ready?"

It was Annis, just coming in at the door, who answered. "Milly says they will be down in five or ten minutes, Cousin Horace. Elsie, shan't we go and put on our wraps?"

As Mrs. Dinsmore was hurrying away, her husband called after her. "My dear, wrap up well, for the night is cold. I have ordered the two closed carriages, but wraps will not come amiss." Then, taking Elsie's hand, he went with her and Annis to their rooms to see that they were warmly clad for the ride.

"We'll have plenty of room in two carriages, won't we?" Annis said as they all gathered in the entrance hall.

"Yes, room enough to avoid crushing the ladies' dresses, I trust," replied Mr. Dinsmore. "Come, Mildred, you, Annis and the doctor step into this one, and my wife, my daughter, and I will take the other."

On reaching Pinegrove, they found the house ablaze with lights and many of the guests already arrived. The ladies were shown to a dressing room where a servant woman was in waiting to help them off with their cloaks and perform any other needed service.

Rose and Mildred here showed themselves not one whit less solicitous about the appearance of the two little girls than in regard to their own. Sashes and stray ringlets were readjusted, and each trim little figure was subjected to a careful scrutiny to make certain that the best effect was secured before they descended to the reception rooms.

The young people were in a parlor by themselves, and there Annis and Elsie were conducted by one servant, while another showed the ladies and gentlemen into the drawing room, announcing them by name.

The host and hostess came forward to meet them with cordial greeting, then Mildred, with an emotion of pleasure, found herself beside Mrs. Travilla. She was sure now that the evening would pass pleasantly to her.

There were also many other intelligent, agreeable people present, and the room was soon full of the hum of many voices conversing in tones more or less subdued.

Mr. Travilla sauntered round the room chatting with one and another of his many friends and acquaintances, then passed into that appropriated to the children. They all seemed to be very merry.

His entrance was greeted with applause from the boys and looks of delight on the part of the girls, for he was a general favorite.

"Will you allow me take this vacant seat by your side, little lady?" he asked, addressing Elsie.

"Oh, yes indeed, sir! I shall be happy to have you do so," she returned, looking up into his face with one of her sweetest smiles.

"What is the game?" he asked. "May I take part in it?"

"It's consequences, and we're having fine fun. Of course we'll be glad to have you join us, sir," answered several voices.

So he stayed and took part in that and several

succeeding games, apparently enjoying the sport as thoroughly as the youngest of them all.

When the time came for the refreshments to be served, he conducted Elsie and Annis to the supper room and waited upon them there.

Elsie was glad her father happened to be so near at hand as to be able to tell her what she might eat, and Annis was wise enough to follow her cousin's example in avoiding rich and indigestible food.

Their party was among the first to leave, yet it was so late that the two mothers felt anxious about their babes, and the little girls were conscious of fatigue, Elsie especially so.

Her father perceived it with concern as she came down from the dressing room and he caught sight of the pale, tired little face half concealed by her hood.

He handed Rose to the carriage, then lifted Elsie tenderly and placed her in it, seated himself by her side, and took her in his arms.

"There, darling, lay your head down on father's shoulder," he said. "You must go to bed as soon as we get home and lie there as long as you like tomorrow morning. There shall be no lessons, nothing to prevent my tired little girl from taking all the rest she needs."

"Papa, you're so good to me!" she murmured, dropping asleep almost before the words had left her lips.

Chapter XIX

Dear as the vital warmth that feeds my life,
Dear as these eyes that weep in fondness o'er thee.

—Thoms Otway

"She is very weary, poor darling!" Rose said softly.

"Yes," her husband answered in the same low tones. "She is perfectly healthy, I think, but not of a vigorous constitution naturally, and she has never fully recovered her strength since—that long and terrible illness."

His voice was tremulous with emotion as he referred to that time of trial—those long-past days so full of grief, anxiety, and remorse that their memory must ever be painful to him.

"I fear I hardly did right in allowing this dissipation," he went on after a moment's pause, "but I thought her better able to bear it."

"Do not be too anxious and troubled, my dear husband," Rose said in a gentle, affectionate tone, laying her hand lightly on his arm. "I think the dear child will be quite restored by a few hours of sound, refreshing sleep. And I am sure she has enjoyed the evening greatly. I caught sight of her face several times, and it was so bright and happy! So, do not reproach yourself, because you did not deny her this pleasure."

"My dear wife! My sweet comforter!" he said. "How is it with you? Are you much fatigued?"

"Oh, no! Only enough so to feel that home and bed will be enjoyable when reached. I have had a very pleasant evening and hope you can say the same."

"Yes, it is pleasant to meet one's friends and acquaintances in that way now and then."

Elsie awoke only partially when the carriage stopped at their own door, and her father carried her to her room in his arms.

"Get her to bed as quickly as you can, Aunt Chloe," he said, "and in the morning darken the room and keep her asleep as long as possible. Annis, my dear,"he said, turning to her, "I fear you too must be very tired?"

"Oh, no, sir, only a little. I think I must be a great deal stronger than Elsie."

"I'm glad to hear it. Well, go to bed now, and don't feel that there is the least occasion to rise from it until you choose."

"That's very kind in you, Cousin Horace." she said, kissing him good night. "I daresay I shall want a good nap in the morning."

She withdrew to her room, wide enough awake to prepare herself for bed.

Mr. Dinsmore stayed and assisted Aunt Chloe in her labors. He could not persuade himself to leave his darling child, until he saw her resting comfortably on her couch. Then he bent over her with a tender caress and a murmured blessing.

"'The Lord bless thee and keep thee. The Lord make his face shine upon thee, and be gracious unto thee. The Lord lift up his countenance upon thee, and give thee peace.'"

"Dear papa," she said, putting her arm about his neck, "that is such a sweet blessing! Doubly sweet because my father asks it of God for me. And may he give it to you, too, dear papa."

She was so tired that she fell asleep again with the last word—"papa"—still trembling on her lips.

Mr. Dinsmore's first act on leaving his room the next morning was to steal softly to Elsie's bedside and bend over her.

She was still sleeping, the sound, refreshing sleep of healthful childhood. The rose had returned to her cheek, and the slightly parted lips were ruby-red. Evidently, she was none the worse for the last night's fatigue, and he turned away with a sigh of relief.

Two hours longer she slept, then awoke to find her father standing close by her side. The full red lips parted in the sweetest of smiles, and the soft dark eyes lifted to his were luminous with love and joy called forth by the fond affection they read in his.

"Good morning, papa!" she said in her sweet, silvery tones. "It is morning, isn't it, though the light is so faint?"

"Yes, I had the room partially darkened so that my tired little girl might sleep off her fatigue."

"Thank you, sir! My dear, kind father! May I get up now?"

"Yes, or will you take your breakfast in bed?"

"I'd rather get up and be dressed first, if you please, papa."

"You are quite rested?"

"Yes, sir, quite. I feel very well."

"I am more thankful than words can express," he sighed, caressing her with hand and lip. "You seemed so completely overcome last night that I have been haunted with the fear that something more than fatigue ailed you."

"My dear papa!" she said again, stroking his face as he leaned over her, "my dear, kind, loving papa! I was only very tired, that was all, and I didn't know I was that till just as I was putting on my wraps to come home. I'd had such a nice time, but all at once, when the fun stopped, I felt as if the strength had all gone out of me."

The murmur of their voices had reached Annis, who was busy dressing.

"Good morning," she said, opening the door a very little and peering in through the crack.

"Good morning," Mr. Dinsmore and Elsie both replied. "Did you sleep well? Do you feel rested?"

"Yes, thank you, I never felt better in my life. But I'm ashamed to have slept so late. Do you know what time it is, Elsie?"

"No."

"Ten o'clock."

Annis's tone was full of a sort of dismayed astonishment. Elsie started up in such haste and sprang out of bed so nimbly that her father laughed to see her.

"No need of such haste, darling," he said, "nor for you to feel troubled, Annis. We older people have only just breakfasted. Aunt Chloe must make haste with your dressing, Elsie, and in the meanwhile, breakfast shall be laid for you and Annis in your boudoir. When you have satisfied your appetite, you may come to me in the study. I will leave you until then."

It was a very delicious little breakfast the children found awaiting them in the pretty boudoir, and they brought to it appetites keen enough to make it most enjoyable.

Then the one went to her father and the other to her sister to spend the next half-hour.

By that time the large, roomy family carriage was at the door. Ladies, gentlemen and children then took a delightful drive, for the sun shone brightly and the air was just cold enough to be pleasant and bracing to mind and body.

It was now the last of November, and from this time until the beginning of the Christmas holidays, ladies and children were much occupied with preparations for them—principally shopping and making up pretty things as Christmas gifts to relatives and friends.

Elsie and Annis were somewhat disposed to neglect lessons for this more fascinating employment, but Mr. Dinsmore would by no means permit it. He was firm in his determination that every task should be thoroughly well learned each day before the fancy work might be touched or a shopping expedition undertaken. Nor would he allow any curtailment of the usual daily outdoor exercise.

They occasionally ventured a slight complaint

that it was very difficult to fix their thoughts on lessons when they were so greatly interested in other things, but he was inexorable.

"It can and must be done," he would say, gently but firmly, addressing his own daughter more particularly. "That a thing which ought to be done is difficult is no reason for excusing ourselves from making the necessary effort to do it. As I have told you before, my child, the determined effort to concentrate your thoughts is excellent mental discipline for you."

He was not very busy at this time and spent some hours each day—generally those in which the children were performing their tasks—reading to his wife and Mildred while they plied the needle, all three in this way renewing their acquaintance most agreeably with Shakespeare, Wordsworth, Scott, Dickens, and other poets and novelists.

The book in hand was generally laid aside when the little girls joined them, but occasionally Mr. Dinsmore read on when he thought the passage unobjectionable even for minds so immature as theirs. Sometimes, too, the books were discussed in their hearing, arousing their interest and curiosity more than their elders realized.

Mr. Dinsmore had always strictly forbidden novels to Elsie, telling her she should read Scott's, Dickens's and others of the better class when he considered her old enough, but not till then.

One evening as they were all gathered in the parlor, Dr. Landreth and Mr. Travilla being among the party also, the talk ran for some time upon the characters and incidents of *Kenilworth* and *Ivanhoe*, then of *Barnaby Rudge*, *Oliver Twist* and *David Copperfield*.

Elsie, seated upon her father's knee, listened with growing interest. "Papa," she whispered, her arm about his neck and her eyes gazing pleadingly into his as a pause in the conversation gave her an opportunity, "mayn't I read those books?"

"Someday, several years from now," he said, softly stroking her hair and smiling into the beseeching eyes.

"Oh, but I mean now, papa! I—"

"No, my child," he said, with grave decision, "they are not suited to your tender years. And as you have no lack of reading matter that interests as well as instructs you, I think my prohibition ought not to be felt as a very severe trial."

Christmas fell on Tuesday that year. Elsie's guests were invited to come to the Oaks for dinner on Monday, the twenty-fourth, and to remain until the following Saturday night. It was her own choice not to have them there on Sunday.

"Because, papa," she said, "you know I should find it very difficult to keep the Sabbath day holy with a company of merry young friends to entertain. Indeed, I'm afraid I could not do it."

"Yes, I fear so, too," he returned. "And besides, you will be, by that time, in need of rest from the care and trouble of entertaining."

Then remembering how ill able she was to bear late hours, he, after a moment's reflection, bade her mention in each note of invitation that the parents need not fear that their children would be injured by loss of necessary sleep, as early hours would be kept except on Christmas eve, and even then their sports should not continue later than ten o'clock.

Her extreme fatigue from the Pinegrove party made him very glad he had taken this precaution. No mother ever watched more tenderly and untiringly over a child's welfare than he over that of this darling only daughter. And no childish heart was ever more full of grateful filial love than Elsie's.

Glowing accounts, heard through the servants, of the grand preparations going on at the Oaks soon made Enna regret her haste in rejecting her brother's invitation, and the regret deepened as time went on, till at length she resolved that she couldn't and wouldn't miss the fun and the feasting in store for Elsie's guests. So, she coaxed and wheedled her mother into writing a note to Mrs. Rose Dinsmore saying they might expect Enna. She would come to dinner on Monday and probably remain through the week.

This note was handed to Rose at the breakfast table on Saturday. She glanced over it, laughed a little, then read it aloud.

Mr. Dinsmore smiled sarcastically, Elsie sighed, and Annis looked provoked. Evidently, Enna would not be the most welcome of the expected guests.

But it was entirely the fault of her own ill temper and selfishness.

"Well, daughter," Mr. Dinsmore said cheerily, for Elsie's sigh, though neither loud nor deep, had reached his ear, "don't let this—shall I say unfortunate?—turn of affairs spoil your pleasure. It may be that Enna will show herself in a new character. At all events we have still two days of grace."

"Oh, yes, sir!" she responded, her face resuming its accustomed sweet and joyous expression, "and I think we'll enjoy our shopping today. I have my list made out, and I hope we'll be able to get everything, because we could hardly take time to go in again on Monday."

"No, certainly not, at least not without tiring you too much, as you expect to have a merry and long evening with your young guests."

"And Monday morning must be devoted to labeling presents and trimming the Christmas tree," remarked Rose.

"How many are going to the city this morning?" asked Mr. Dinsmore.

"All except babies and servants," answered his wife.

"Then shall I order the family carriage to be at the door in fifteen minutes after prayers?"

"Yes, if you please. It will be best to start as early as we can, though our shopping today is not likely to be very arduous, since we have already bought everything the selection of which would require much time and taste."

Mr. Dinsmore remarked that he had directed two of the servants to go into the woods that morning to get the Christmas tree. Then he proposed that it should be set up in a parlor not in constant use, trimmed that evening, and the room door locked until the proper hour of exhibition Monday.

"My dear, I believe yours is the better plan," said Rose. "Do you not think so, Mildred?"

"Yes, decidedly so, if we do not fatigue ourselves too much in the city today."

"Can we help?" the little girls were asking.

"Oh, no!" returned the older people in chorus, "You are to have the pleasure of the surprise of seeing the finished work on Christmas Eve."

"Yes, there is one thing they can do," Mr. Dinsmore remarked. "Label the presents they give to others."

They were well pleased with the suggestion. Indeed, they seemed in a mood to be pleased with everything except the prospect of Enna's company the following week, and that they resolutely refused to contemplate.

They enjoyed their drive, their shopping, the homecoming after it, and the good dinner that followed. Then there was a restful chat among themselves and with the older people—plans for the entertainment and amusement of the expected guests being the staple of discourse—and a romp with the babies.

A gallop about the grounds on the Shetland ponies and the labeling of their presents filled up most of their time for the remainder of the day and evening, and they went early to bed to be ready for the full enjoyment of the coming Lord's day with its sacred duties and pleasures.

CHAPTER XX

Haste thee, my nymph, and bring with thee
Jest and youthful jollity,
Quips and cranks, and wanton wiles,
Nods and becks and wreathed smiles.

—MILTON'S *L'ALLEGRO*

MONDAY CAME—CLEAR, bright, and warm for the season.

"It's as lovely a day as we could have asked for," Annis said, to which Elsie responded, "Yes indeed! I think everybody will come, for no regrets have been sent in, and there is no excuse to be found in either the weather or the state of the roads."

"I don't believe anybody is anxious for an excuse," said Annis. "I haven't a doubt they're all glad you invited them."

All their preparations being already made, the children spent nearly all the morning in out-of-door sports, making the most of the good weather, and coming in just in time to be dressed for dinner at as early an hour as any of the invited guests could be expected.

They all came, both older and younger, ladies and gentlemen, girls and boys—excepting Mr.

and Mrs. Dinsmore of Roselands, who had accepted a prior invitation.

It had been foreseen that in such case the house would be so full that Elsie and Annis would each be constrained to accept a bedfellow, and Annis had expressed a strong preference for sharing Elsie's room and bed, giving up hers to two of the newcomers. And so it was arranged, with Carrie Howard and Lucy Carrington being installed in Annis's room, immediately on their arrival.

They had scarcely taken possession when the Roselands carriage drove up and deposited Adelaide, Walter, and Enna.

"I meant to be among the first," Adelaide said as Rose hastened to meet her at the door with a warm, sisterly greeting, "but Enna delayed us so with her whims and tempers that I presume we are the very last."

"Yes, you are a few minutes behind the Carringtons, who came after everybody else but you. But never mind, it's better late than never, and you are in full time for dinner. Come let me have the pleasure of showing you to your room. I am sorry to have to ask you to take Enna in with you, but we are so full that we have no separate room to offer her."

"There is no need of apology," Adelaide returned good humoredly, "and I think it is a much better plan than it would be to put her with anyone else. Come, Enna, you are to go with me. Didn't you hear?"

"Yes, but what if I don't choose to?" the child answered with a pout.

"In that case, you can return by the way you came," said Mr. Dinsmore, appearing on the scene. "How do you do, Adelaide?"

"Very well, thank you," she said, moving on down the hall with him and Rose, leaving Enna to follow or not as she pleased.

Enna hung back, muttering that she "wouldn't stay to be abused and treated like a nobody."

"No, don't," Walter teased. "Stand on your dignity and go home. I wish you would, for I know we'll have a great deal better time without you."

"You hateful boy! I shan't go one step!" she exclaimed, stamping her foot at him and rushing after Adelaide and the others.

"I say, En," he called after her with a grin, "you'd better be on your good behavior, or Santa Claus will pass you by."

"Marse Walter, shall I show you to yo' room, sah?" asked a servant who had all this time stood waiting.

"Yes, Dick, I suppose I'd better see if I'm all right for dinner."

"Now, Enna," Adelaide said, turning to the pouting child as the door of their room closed upon Mr. and Mrs. Dinsmore, leaving them alone together, "you must behave yourself decently or you shall go home at once, whether you will or no."

Enna was by no means willing to miss the fun and gifts or the feasting which she knew were in store for those who should share the hospitalities of the Oaks for the next few days. And being well aware that Adelaide was quite capable of carrying out her threat, especially if assisted by their Brother Horace, she reluctantly decided to banish her ill humor and submit quietly, if not quite pleasantly, to the arrangements that had been made for her.

Going down to the drawing room, they found the whole company of old and young gathered there, and presently dinner was announced.

It was a grand affair of many courses, and when they left the table, the short winter day was drawing to a close. There was no wine upon the table, for the Dinsmores of the Oaks were strictly temperate in principle and practice, but the most fragrant and delicious coffee was served with the last course.

After that, the gentlemen who did not smoke withdrew with the ladies to the drawing room, the lads went out into the grounds to amuse themselves there until dark, and Elsie, taking the little girls to her apartments, showed them her baby-house, with its family of dolls, a number of other costly toys, a cabinet of curiosities, books, and pictures. There was no lack of material for their entertainment, and tongues ran fast as they talked of what they were handling and of the Christmas gifts they had received before leaving home or expected to have sent them tomorrow.

As Elsie's doting father was constantly adding to her store of pretty things, there were some which were new even to Enna.

She regarded them with curiosity at first, then with an envious eye, in sullen silence for a time. But at length, during a pause in the conversation, she remarked, "I don't think it's fair, Elsie, that you should have so much more of everything nice than anybody else has."

"I do, then!" exclaimed Carrie Howard. "Because she's so nice herself! Besides, I know that with all her blessings, she's had her trials, too."

"What?" cried Enna snappishly.

"You for one," returned Carrie, laughing.

"Thank you, Miss Howard, but I don't belong to her," snapped Enna, growing very red and angry.

This sally was greeted with a general laugh, which only had the effect to increase Enna's anger, though Elsie did not join in it.

"Don't be vexed, Enna, they are only teasing you a little," she said in a gentle, persuasive tone. "I wouldn't mind it."

"But I will! And I shan't stay here to be insulted! I believe you just put them up to it, you hateful thing!" And the angry child marched out of the room, holding her head high, as she had seen her mother do when similarly affected.

Everybody felt relieved, and the mirthful chat and light, careless laughter were resumed.

Elsie alone was slightly disturbed by Enna's behavior. She was somewhat abstracted for a moment while considering the question whether what had occurred was of such a nature that she must report it to her father in obedience to his command. But having decided in the negative, she recovered her accustomed sweet serenity and gave her whole attention to promoting the enjoyment of her remaining guests.

"Girls," she said presently, "wouldn't you like to see my baby brother and Cousin Mildred's little Percy?"

Elsie led the way to the nursery, where they found the little fellows, each in the arms of his mother and in a state of mind and condition of dress to show off to advantage.

Elsie had taken herself to the drawing room, and in answer to Adelaide's query why she had left her mates, asserted that they were all as cross and hateful as they could be.

"Ah," returned Adelaide indifferently. "Well, I have noticed that the people are very apt to get a return of the treatment they give." And with that, she resumed her chat with a lady sitting on her other side, and left Enna to amuse herself as she best could.

The child found it dull enough sitting there, or wandering about the room unnoticed, but was too proud to go back to the society of those she had left in a huff.

Herbert Carrington, Lucy's twin brother, was the only other child in the room just then. He sat at a window overlooking that part of the grounds where the other boys were sporting and was watching them with wistful eyes, probably feeling the lameness which prevented him from joining them a sore trial. But he was patient sufferer and very seldom uttered a word of complaint.

Elsie, in Enna's place, would have gone to him and tried to cheer and entertain him, but the latter only looked toward him and turned away with a face of disgust, despising the poor lad for the physical infirmity which was not his fault but his sad misfortune.

But it began to grow dark, lamps were lighted, and the boys came in.

The children were growing eager for the opening of the doors to the room where the Christmas tree was, and some of the older people were somewhat impatient to see it and to learn the nature of the fruits it bore. All were ready to accept the invitation to do so on leaving the tea table.

It was a fine, large tree reaching from floor to ceiling, with wide spreading branches almost bending beneath the weight of glittering ornaments, toys, candies, fruits, and many more costly things.

When there had been sufficient time for everybody to see and thoroughly appreciate its present appearance, the work of distribution began, Mr. Travilla taking down the presents, calling aloud the name on each, and Mr. and Mrs. Dinsmore and Adelaide handing them to the owners.

No one—member of the family, guest, or servant—had been forgotten or neglected. The gifts had been carefully chosen to suit the circumstances and tastes of each recipient and seemed to afford very general satisfaction. Even Enna could for once find no cause or excuse for grumbling, having received a pair of very beautiful bracelets from Elsie; necklace, pin, and earrings to match from Mr. Dinsmore and Rose; besides some smaller gifts from other relatives.

Fortunately, she did not know that some of Elsie's presents, in particular a set of pink coral— necklace and bracelets—from her father, and an opal ring from Mr. Travilla, were far more costly than her own.

Annis thought she fared wonderfully well, receiving a pair of gold bracelets from Elsie, a gold chain for her neck from Mr. Dinsmore, and a gold locket enameled with blue forget-me-nots from Mildred, and also, a pearl ring from Mr. Travilla, one set with a topaz from Dr. Landreth, and a dozen beautiful handkerchiefs from Rose.

The other gifts of jewelry were a moonstone ring to Mildred from her husband and a sardonyx from Mr. Dinsmore to Rose.

These four happening to be grouped together with Mr. Travilla, Annis, and Elsie, Mildred said, looking down at her new ring, which her husband had just slipped upon her finger, "This is very pretty, my dear, but had you any motive for selecting this particular kind of stone? Precious stones are said to have a language as well as flowers, are they not?"

"Yes, and moonstone is said to protect from harm and danger," returned the doctor laughingly.

"And sardonyx?" asked Rose.

"Insures conjugal felicity," replied her husband with a fond look into her sweet face.

"Oh, Mr. Travilla! What's the language of this—opal is it?" asked Elsie.

"Yes, my little friend, it is an opal, and it is said to denote hope and to sharpen the faith and sight of the possessor."

"Thank you!" she exclaimed heartily, gazing down at it with a pleased, happy face.

"And what is the language of pearls?" asked Annis, looking admiringly at hers.

"Purity, and they are said to give clearness to both physical and mental vision."

"Oh, I like that!" she said, "and I think you were very, very kind to give it to me."

Elsie had stolen close to her father's side and slipped one hand into his.

He bent down to look smilingly into her eyes and give her a gentle kiss.

"Papa," she said softly, "thank you very much for your lovely present."

"Welcome, my darling, and many thanks to you for my beautiful present from you."

It was a small but very fine painting by one of the old masters. She had given a beautiful lace set—collar and under sleeves—to her mamma and one to Mildred.

The presents having all been distributed, the ladies and gentlemen adjourned to the drawing room, leaving the children in possession of the parlor where the tree stood.

"Let's play games!" cried a chorus of voices in which several boyish ones were conspicuous.

Elsie asked what they would have, suggesting a number of the quieter kind, but none of those seemed to suit. Evidently, the majority at least were in a romping mood.

"Hot—butter—beans," proposed Walter. "That's good fun and needn't be very noisy, either."

No dissenting voices being raised, Elsie asked, "What shall we hide?"

"Here's a mouse made of gray flannel," said

Annis, taking it from where it lay at the foot of the tree. "I should think that it would do very well."

"Yes, and as you have it in your hand, you will hide it first."

"Yes, if nobody else wants to. Now, all cover your eyes, please, and don't look till I say, 'Hot— butter—beans! Please to come to supper.'"

The game was continued for some time with the understanding that the hiding must be done in that room. Then, as the good places seemed to have all been used, they took in the next room and the spacious entrance hall beyond.

At length, Elsie was the finder, and it became her turn to hide the mouse. With it in her hand, she stole softly into the hall and glanced around from floor to ceiling.

It was a very large and handsome apartment, the ceiling lofty, the floor of tessellated marble, the walls frescoed and adorned with two or three fine paintings and several pieces of choice statuary.

Glancing up at one of those last, occupying a niche several feet above the floor, the child thought what a good hiding place for the mouse might be made of that niche. She could surely slip the little thing in behind the feet of the statue, where it could not be seen, and who would ever think of looking for it there?

She was not tall enough to reach up to the place while standing on the floor, so she softly moved a chair near and stepped upon it.

Even then she could not reach easily, not with- out standing on the edge of the chair, and just as she seemed to have attained her object, it slipped from under her. She caught wildly at the statue to save herself from falling, and she and it came down together with a terrible crash upon the marble floor.

CHAPTER XXI

At Christmas play, and make good cheer,
For Christmas comes but once a year.

—TUSSER

THE WHOLE HOUSE was aroused and terrified by the sudden crashing sound, succeeded by perfect stillness, and members of the family, guests, and servants came rushing into the hall, most of them in wild excitement, not knowing but the next thing might be the falling in of the roof or the tumbling of the walls about their ears.

Mr. Dinsmore, who was standing near the drawing room door at that end of the hall, was the foremost of the crowd and saw with a thrill of terror and despair his darling only daughter lying apparently insensible upon the floor, killed, he thought, by the crushing weight of the statue, which seemed to rest upon her prostrate form.

In an instant, he was at her side, his terror somewhat abated as he perceived that it had missed her, though by but a hair's breadth, and that she was making an effort to rise.

"My child! My darling!" he said tremulously, stooping over her and gently raising her in his arms. "Are you much hurt?"

"No, papa, not much I think," she murmured faintly, for the fall had partially stunned her. "But, oh, papa, I've broken your lovely statue, and I'm so sorry!"

"Never mind that! What do I care for it in comparison with you?" he said almost indignantly, making his way through the crowd of frightened, anxious guests and servants.

"Is she much hurt?"

"How did it happen?"

"How did she come to fall?" everybody was asking of her father or of each other as they fell back from the drawing room door to let him enter.

He did not seem to hear or heed them; his attention was wholly occupied with her.

"Am I giving you pain?" he asked in tenderest tones.

"Very little," she answered, and her voice sounded quite natural now.

He sat down with her on a sofa, Rose, Mildred, Mr. Landreth, and Mr. Travilla gathering round.

"Where are you hurt, dear child?" the doctor asked.

"Only my knee, sir, and I don't think it's more than bruised," she said, looking up into his face with a faint smile. "I'm ashamed to have frightened you all so."

But her head dropped on her father's shoulder as she spoke, and she grew deathly pale.

Her father's face reflected the pallor of hers as the thought darted into his mind that she might have received some internal injury.

"She is faint from the shock to her nervous system," the doctor said. "Better carry her to her room and lay her on her bed."

The advice was followed at once, her father lifting her again in his arms and carrying her as gently and tenderly as possible, the doctor and Rose following at his request.

The last named soon returned to the drawing room, where the guests were waiting in almost silent expectancy, with the good news that the doctor found no serious injury. The shock of the fall and a few not very bad bruises were all he could discover. He thought she would be about again the next day.

Rose added that Mr. Dinsmore wished to be excused for a short time and hoped they would enjoy themselves as if nothing had happened to disturb them.

"I should have her put to bed at once and get to sleep as soon as possible," Dr. Landreth said as he left Elsie's room.

"Yes, it shall be done," Mr. Dinsmore answered. "Aunt Chloe, undress her immediately. I will help you. There, put these away carefully," he said, handing her the necklace and bracelets he just unclasped from his daughter's neck and arms. Turning to Elsie, he said, "Keep as quiet as you can, dearest, and let papa and mammy do it all."

"Dear papa, you seem to have no reproof at all for me!" she said, looking lovingly into his eyes.

"That can wait till tomorrow," he answered with playful look and tone. "I am sorry for my little girl that her Christmas eve should be so spoiled for her," he added presently, giving her a tender caress.

"But it was my own fault, papa, and I'm afraid I've spoiled yours and other people's too."

"Well, well, accidents will happen, and you shall tell me all about it tomorrow, if you feel equal to the task. Now I shall sit beside you until you go to sleep."

"How nice, papa!" she exclaimed. "It more than pays for my slight hurts and my fright, for, oh, I was frightened when I felt myself falling."

"There! Don't talk about it anymore tonight," he said, holding her close to his heart for an instant, then laying her in her bed.

"Papa, must I say my prayers in bed?"

"For tonight I think you must. And they need not be very long; we are not heard for our much speaking."

It was not long before she slept, and until then, he sat beside the bed, holding her hand in his and singing softly one of her favorite hymns.

Then, enjoining the old nurse to watch her carefully, and if she woke and seemed in pain, to send at once for him, he returned to his guests.

He wanted her without a bedfellow that night so that he might feel free to go to her when he would. Thus, Annis occupied a couch in Mildred's dressing room.

Elsie was still sleeping sweetly when her father came in and stood by her bed the last thing before seeking his own, and he always found her so when he stole softly in again two or three times during the night.

She woke at her usual hour in the morning, and hearing him moving quietly about in the next room, called softly to him, "Merry Christmas, dear papa."

"Ah, my darling, a merry Christmas and happy New Year to you!" he responded, coming quickly to her side. "You are looking very bright," he added joyously, bending down to kiss forehead, lips, cheeks, and eyes. "Do you feel no ill effects from your fall?"

"No, sir. May I get up now, and come to you in the study when I am dressed?"

"Yes, if you feel quite able. Aunt Chloe," he said as the old nurse came in, "bring Miss Elsie a glass of good, rich iced milk and let her drink it before she rises."

"Yes, sah, I'se do dat berry ting," returned Aunt Chloe. "How is you, honey? Well 'nuff to get out ob bed dis Christmas mornin'?"

"Yes, mammy, but why don't you catch me? Aren't you afraid you'll miss your Christmas gift?"

"Yah, yah, chile, not a bit! 'Spect you's got it all ready an' couldn't keep it from your ole mammy ef you tried. Now I'se off after dat milk. But fust, I hopes, darlin', you'll hab de merriest of Christmases and de happiest New Year de good Lord eber give you."

"Thank you, dear mammy, and may you have the same," Elsie responded, looking affectionately after her nurse as she hurried from the room.

Her father stayed with her till he had seen her drain the glass of sweet rich milk which Aunt Chloe brought, then left her to be dressed.

Going through the hall on the way to his study, he passed the scene of last night's accident. The statue had been replaced in its niche by the servants, but it was a wreck, the nose crushed, an arm and a foot broken.

He had valued it in the past, but his only emotion as he glanced at it now was one of heartfelt thankfulness that it had fallen beside rather than upon his child.

Half an hour later, she came to him looking so bright and happy, so sweet and fair, that his pulses bounded with joy at the sight.

She ran into his outstretched arms, put hers about his neck, and pressed her sweet lips to his again and again. "Dear, dear papa, how I love you!" she said, laying her soft cheek to his. "I do believe almost any other father would have scolded and punished me last night."

"Not a father who loved you as I do. But how did it all happen? I cannot think what you could have been doing there."

Then she told him all about it, adding, "I saw the statue just now and it is quite ruined. Oh, papa, I am so sorry!"

"Never mind that. If this accident teaches you a lesson on the folly and danger of climbing up and reaching in that way—such a lesson that you will never try it again—I shall not mourn over the loss but will consider your safety cheaply purchased by it. But do you know what you have brought on yourself by this escapade?"

"What, papa?" she asked with a startled look. His tone was so grave it half frightened her.

"Your father's presence with you and your mates whenever there is any romping game to be played."

"Oh," she cried, clapping her hands, "that will be so nice! And will you join us in the games?"

"Perhaps. Now let us have our reading. I have chosen the sweet story of our Saviour's birth and the visit of the angels to the shepherds as the most appropriate to the day."

"Yes, papa, surely it is," she said, a sweet, tender gravity overspreading her lovely countenance while the soft eyes were luminous with love and joy. "I have been thinking of it all the morning and thanking God in my heart for the gift of his dear Son. And this is my verse for today: 'God so loved the world, that he gave his only begotten Son, that whosoever believeth in him should not perish, but have everlasting life.' Oh, papa, isn't that a sweet, sweet verse, and wasn't it wonderful love?"

A little before the breakfast hour, Mr. Dinsmore and Elsie went to the drawing room, where they found Rose, Mildred, and Annis.

No one else was there at the moment, though very soon Dr. Landreth and Mr. Travilla came in, then one guest after another until nearly all were present.

The two ladies and Annis embraced Elsie in turn, saying how glad they were to see her looking so well in spite of her accident and how alarmed about her they had been.

"Are you quite sure that you feel none the worse for it?" asked Rose.

"No, mamma. I am so very sorry to have broken that lovely statue."

"It is a pity," Rose said with a slight smile, "but I am sure your papa does not want you to grieve in the very least over it, and my query referred altogether to bodily injury."

"Please excuse me, mamma," Elsie said, "I'm afraid my misunderstanding was partly willful. I have a few bruises, but they scarcely hurt me unless they are touched."

Inquiries, condolences, and Christmas greetings and good wishes were showered upon her as the other visitors gathered in, until at length Enna remarked with a disdainful toss of the head, "Dear me, Elsie, what a fuss everybody does make over you, just because you had a trifling accident—a fall off a chair!"

"A fall off a chair, Miss Enna," said Mr. Travilla, "has sometimes proved to be a very serious affair. And if that statue had fallen on, instead of alongside, our little friend, it would without doubt have broken some of her bones, if nothing worse."

"I'm glad it didn't then. 'Twould have spoiled all our fun, for of course Horace would have sent us all home at once."

"Well, Enna, one thing can be said in your praise—that you are no hypocrite!" exclaimed Carrie Howard with a scornful curl of the lip. "If you are utterly heartless, you don't try to hide it with a pretense of sensibility and kindness."

"You are well answered and reproved for once, Enna," remarked Mr. Dinsmore with grave displeasure and disgust.

The morning was so fine that the family and

guests spent the greater part of it in the open air, riding, driving, or walking. Elsie generously gave up her phaeton to Carrie and Lucy—the other little girls to take their turn afterward—and the larger ponies to the boys, but her father and Mr. Travilla drove her and Annis out in the carriage of the latter.

There was a great deal of candy about, everyone having received a box of it when the gifts were distributed, and some of the little people ate so much that evening and on getting up in the morning that they brought little appetite to their breakfast, but Elsie had not yet tasted it.

"What is that?" her father asked, seeing a paper parcel in her hand as she came out to take her drive.

"My box of candy, papa. I thought it would be nice to hand round to you all, and perhaps you would let me eat some, too. I haven't had any at all yet."

"Yes," he said, handing her into the carriage, "you may eat a little now and shall have a larger quantity after dinner."

"Cousin Horace," remarked Annis, who was already seated in the carriage, "I do think Elsie is the best girl in the world! I don't believe I could have resisted the temptation to taste a little candy, when everybody around me was eating it, as she did last night."

"Yes," he said, looking fondly at his little girl, "she is a good, obedient child."

Elsie's face flushed with pleasure at his words, and her eyes sparkled.

Of course, there was a grand Christmas dinner at the Oaks, where, in addition to a great variety of toothsome viands, there was, "the feast of reason and the flow of soul."

Innocent pleasures were provided in abundance for the afternoon and evening of that day and all the others to the end of the week: intellectual conversation, music of a high order, tableaux vivans, acting of charades, and others too numerous to mention.

There was very little jarring among the participants, old or young. Enna behaved uncommonly well, probably because either Mr. Dinsmore or Mr. Travilla was almost always present, and often both were. And in their occasional absences, Rose, Adelaide, or Mildred was sure to be near enough to see and hear all that went on.

Thus, Elsie was secured from ill usage and from being burdened with the responsibility of providing amusement for her guests.

Both she and Annis enjoyed the week greatly yet felt a sense of relief when on Saturday evening the last of their guests had departed, leaving them to the full enjoyment of each other's society and that of the usual quiet home circle. The older guests had gone, too, with the exception of Adelaide and Mr. and Mrs. Travilla, but they seemed almost to belong to the family.

CHAPTER XXII

How firm a foundation, ye saints of the Lord,
Is laid for your faith in his excellent word!
What more can he say than to you he hath said,
You who unto Jesus for refuge hath fled.

— KIRKHAM

"THE LAST SUNDAY of the old year!" Mrs. Travilla said in a meditative tone, more as if thinking aloud than addressing her companions.

It was evening, and all the family at the Oaks were gathered about the fire in the parlor usually occupied by them when alone. It was not so large as the drawing room and seemed cozier for a small company.

"Yes, a solemn thought," said Rose. "The last Sunday and the last hours of the old year seem most appropriate times for a glance backward at the path we have already trod and forward over that which still lies before."

"Yes, looking back to see wherein we have stepped aside out of the straight and narrow way that leads to eternal life, and forward with the resolve that with God's help we will walk more steadily in it, that we will run in the way of His commandments." It was Mildred who spoke.

"And not at our shortcomings only," resumed the old lady, "but also at God's great mercies in the past and all His great and precious promises for the future. 'Lo, I am with you always, even unto the end of the world.' 'I will never leave thee nor forsake thee.' 'And even to your old age I am He, and even to hoar hairs I will carry you.' 'This god is our God forever and ever, He will be our guide even unto death.'

"I want to testify to you all tonight that in a life of threescore and ten I have found him ever faithful to his promises. Goodness and mercy have followed me all the days of my life thus far, and shall surely do so to the very end.

"I have not been without trials—many and sometimes very sore, having seen the grave close over a beloved husband and five dear children—but He has sustained me under them all. Oh, it is in the darkest hours the star of His wondrous love shines forth in its greatest power and splendor, and we learn the sweetness of resting wholly upon Him! As my days, so has my strength been, because the eternal God was my refuge, and underneath were the everlasting arms."

"Ah!" said Mildred, breaking the silence that had fallen upon them with the last words of her dear old friend, "All we want to make us supremely happy is faith enough to believe every word our Master says, to trust Him fully with both our temporal and spiritual interests, and to keep all His sweet commands."

"Such as what, love?" asked her husband softly, sitting close by her side.

"I was thinking of the opening verses of the forty-third chapter of Isaiah," she answered. "In the first and second verses he says, 'O Israel, fear not; for I have redeemed thee; I have called thee by thy name; thou art mine. When thou passeth through the waters, I will be with thee; and through the rivers, they shall not overflow thee; when thou walkest through the fire, thou shalt not be burned, neither shall the flame kindle upon thee.'

"And again in the fifth, 'Fear not, for I am with thee.' Could we miss being happy if we fully obeyed so much as this one command, 'Fear not,' and fully believed and trusted in these precious promises?"

"I think not," said Mr. Dinsmore. "And what right have we to disobey in being afraid of any-thing—loss, accident, sickness, death, the enmity and malice of temporal or spiritual foes—when he bids us fear not? And again he says, 'Be care-ful for nothing.' 'Take no thought for your life, what ye shall eat, or what ye shall drink, nor yet for your body, what ye shall put on.'"

He paused, and Mrs. Travilla added another quotation.

"'But seek ye first the kingdom of God and His righteousness, and all these things shall be added unto you.'"

"And," said Rose, "Paul tells us, 'Godliness is profitable unto all things, having promise of the life that now is, and of that which is to come.'"

"Papa," said Elsie, "mayn't we see how many of these little commandments we can remember?"

"Shall we?" he asked, glancing around the small circle.

All agreed that it would be a pleasant and profitable exercise, and Mrs. Travilla, as the oldest person present, began, the others following as a text occurred to them.

"'My son, give me thy heart.'"

"'Come unto me,' the word of Jesus," Rose said, "and He bids us bring to Him others who have need of healing. 'Bring him hither to me,' He said of the boy who had a dumb and deaf spirit. 'Let him that heareth say come.'"

"And having come," said Mildred, "we are to be strong in the Lord and in the power of His might, and to grow in grace and in the knowledge of our Lord and Saviour Jesus Christ."

"'Casting all your care upon Him, for He careth for you.'" was the doctor's text.

Then Mr. Travilla: "'Not slothful in business; fervent in spirit, serving the Lord.'"

Mr. Dinsmore's: "'Rejoicing in hope; patient in tribulation; continuing instant in prayer.'"

Elsie's: "'A new commandment I give unto you, that ye love one another: as I loved you, that ye also love one another.'"

Annis repeated: "'Love as brethren, be pitiful, be courteous.'"

Adelaide: "'In lowliness of mind let each esteem other better than themselves.'"

Then it went round again.

"'Let patience have her perfect work.'"

"'Set your affection on things above, not on things on the earth.'"

"'Let your conversation be without covetousness, and be content with such things as ye have.'"

"'Be not forgetful to entertain strangers.'"

"'Use hospitality one to another without grudging.'"

"'As we have there opportunity, let us do good unto all men, especially unto them who are of the household of faith.'"

"'Children, obey your parents in the Lord: for this is right. Honor thy father and mother.'" This came from Elsie's lips, and as she repeated the command, her arm crept lovingly around her father's neck, for she was, as usual, close at his side.

"'Fight the good fight of faith, lay hold on eternal life,'" Annis repeated.

Then Mrs. Travilla: "'Let us run with patience the race that is set before us.'"

Rose: "'In everything give thanks.'"

Mildred: "'Ye believe in God, believe also in me.'"

Dr. Landreth: "'Bear ye one another's burdens.'"

Mr. Travilla: "'Rejoice with them that do rejoice, and weep with them that weep.'"

Adelaide: "'Comfort ye, comfort ye, my people, saith your God.'"

Mr. Dinsmore: "'Provide things honest in the sight of all men.'"

Dr. Landreth: "'Every man shall bear his own burden.'"

A slight pause followed the last text, and then Mrs. Travilla broke the silence.

"In all these and many more we learn His will concerning us," she said, "and He tells us, 'If ye love me, keep my commandments.' 'He that hath my commandments and keepeth them, he it is that loveth me.' Obedience—to a parent, and God is our Father; to a Master, and Jesus is our Lord and Master—is the test of love.

"'We love him because he first loved us,' and obey him not that we may be saved but because we *are* saved.

"'Verily, verily, I say unto you, He that heareth my word, and believeth on him that sent me, hath everlasting life, and shall not come into condemnation; but is passed from death unto life.'

"'Looking unto Jesus'—trusting in Him alone for salvation, trying to be like Him, and to know, to do, and suffer all His holy will—this is what it is to be a Christian, a follower of God, not as a slave but as a dear child. 'Be ye therefore followers of God as dear children.'"

"'Whosoever shall do the will of God, the same is my brother, and my sister and mother,'" read Mr. Dinsmore from his open Bible.

"Let us search out something more in regard to that will."

"Please read the fourth and fifth verses of the first chapter of Ephesians," said Mrs. Travilla.

He turned to it and read: "'According as he hath chosen us in him before the foundation of the world, that we should be holy and without blame before him in love: Having predestinated us unto the adoption of children by Jesus Christ to himself, according to the good pleasure of his will.'"

"What a blessed will!" she commented, "to predestinate us to the adoption of children—Us! Rebels against His authority, enemies by wicked works. And then it was His will to give His only begotten and well-beloved Son to die that we might live. He said, 'Lo, I come to do thy will, O God.'"

"'And this is the will of God, even your sanctification,'" quoted Mildred. "What Christian heart but must rejoice in that!"

Then Rose read: "'And this is the father's will which hath sent me, that of all which he hath given me I should lose nothing, but should raise it up again at the last day. And this is the will of him that sent me, that every one which seeth the Son, and believeth on him, may have everlasting life: and I will raise him up at the last day.' Oh!" she exclaimed. "Shall we not rejoice in His will?"

Mr. Travilla's Bible lay open before him. "Here," he said, "in second Peter, third chapter and ninth verse, we read, 'The Lord is not slack concerning his promise, as some men count slackness, but is long suffering to us-ward, not willing that any should perish, but that all should come to repentance.'"

Then turning to Ezekiel, eighteenth chapter, "'Cast away from you all your transgressions, whereby ye have transgressed, and make you a new heart and a new spirit, for why will ye die, O house of Israel? For I have no pleasure in the death of him that dieth, saith the Lord God: wherefore turn yourselves and live ye.'"

Chapter XXIII

When I am filled with sore distress
For some surprising sin,
I'll plead thy perfect righteousness
And mention none but thine.

— WATTS

THE NEXT DAY, the little party at the Oaks was greatly reduced in size, Mr. Travilla and his mother having gone to their own home, and the doctor, Mildred, and Annis to pay a visit of a week to some relative of his living in the next county, so that Adelaide was the only remaining guest.

Elsie missed Annis very much, especially when alone in her own apartments. Therefore, she spent most of her time with Rose and Adelaide or in her papa's study. She liked to be with him better than anywhere else, even when he was too busy to notice her and must not be spoken to, and he was always pleased to have her by his side. She had the freedom of his study, too, whether he were there or not.

Regular lessons were not to go on during Annis's absence, but Elsie read history with her father for an hour every morning and spent another over her music and drawing.

On Monday, the last day of the old year, as she sat on his knee after their early morning reading and prayer together, he told her that "tomorrow evening—New Year's night," the Carletons were to give a large party, similar to the one they had attended at Pinegrove. "And we are all invited to it," he added.

Her face flushed with pleasure. "Will you let me go, papa?" she asked, and he read in her eyes that she was very desirous to do so.

"I have something to say to you before I answer that question," he said, softly stroking her hair and looking with grave tenderness into the beseeching eyes. "You are not very strong and bore the fatigue of the Pinegrove party so ill that I fear the effect upon your health if I should allow you to attend another.

"Health is one of God's good gifts, and as such we have no right to throw it away simply for our own pleasure. It is a Christian duty to take care of it because we can serve God better with strong, healthy bodies than with feeble, sickly ones. The Bible bids us, 'Whether therefore ye eat or drink, or whatsoever ye do, do all to the glory of God.' Do you think, my child, that you can obey this command in going to the party, when you know it is likely to injure your health?"

"I'm afraid not, papa," she answered, in a low, reluctant tone.

"Very well, I leave it to your own conscience. You shall decide yourself, whether you go or stay."

"Then I shall stay, papa, because you have made it plain to me that I ought to. But," she sighed, "it will seem very lonesome while you and mamma are gone."

"No, we will not go early, and I shall see you safe in your bed before starting."

"Then I shall not care so much," she said. "I am pretty sure to go to sleep as soon as my head touches the pillow. Papa, are we to have any company tomorrow?"

"None by invitation. The house has been so full for some time that your mamma and I feel that it will be pleasant to take our New Year's dinner with only our own little family, for we hardly consider your aunt Adelaide as other than one of ourselves."

"I think it will be nice," she said with satisfaction, "though I'd be glad if we could have Cousin Milly and the doctor and Annis."

"So should I," he responded. "They have come to seem a part of our family."

So, New Year's day passed very quietly at the Oaks yet very pleasantly, too. Elsie received some handsome presents from her papa, Rose, Adelaide, and Mr. Travilla. She enjoyed that and also presenting the gifts she had prepared for them.

Her father rode out with her shortly after breakfast, and on their return they found Mr. Travilla in the drawing room making his New Year's call. There were several other gentlemen doing the same, and indeed there was quite a stream of callers all the morning.

Refreshments were offered to all—cake, candies, fruits, lemonade, and hot coffee—all of the finest, but no wine or other intoxicating beverage.

Elsie was allowed a little cake, a little candy,

and as much fruit and lemonade as she wished. She was well content with these and with the pleasure of listening to the talk and watching the callers come and go.

Mr. Travilla devoted himself a part of the time to entertainment, and that was something she always enjoyed greatly.

"Are you going to the party tonight?" he asked.

Elsie shook her head. "Papa thinks I could not bear the fatigue without injury to my health, so it wouldn't be right for me to go. But he left it to my conscience, he said, and let me decide for myself."

"Did he, indeed?" Mr. Travilla seemed both surprised and pleased. "Well," he said, "I think you were very right and wise to decide as you did."

Elsie thought it very kind of her father to let her decide for herself and also to promise not to leave her until she was in bed for the night. In the fullness of her gratitude, she offered to go to bed an hour earlier than usual.

"Dear child!" Rose exclaimed. "That would be asking quite too much of you, and we really don't care to be among the first arrivals."

"No," remarked Adelaide, "we'll be there long enough if we are the very last. I'm growing tired of parties."

Mr. Dinsmore had not responded to Elsie's proposition as yet, except by a pleased smile and tender caress.

"It would be no great sacrifice, mamma," Elsie said, "for somehow I feel pretty tired tonight. Papa and I took quite a long walk this afternoon, and I'm not sorry now that I'm to stay at home."

"Home is a good place for tired people, isn't it, daughter, and bed the best part of it?" her father said, repeating his caresses. "So, I accept your generous offer and shall be glad to see you in bed at the early hour you have named."

"Well," said Adelaide, "I suppose if we go early we need not stay very late."

"There is no need for you to go any earlier than you wish," said her brother. "I shall order the carriage for whatever hour you and Rose fix upon."

"Mamma and auntie, I'd like to see you when you are dressed," Elsie said, "but, I suppose, that won't be till I'm in bed."

Both ladies promised to come into her bedroom and exhibit themselves before donning their wraps. They came in together and found her already in bed but not asleep.

"Oh!" she cried, sitting up to take a good view. "How nice and pretty you both look! I hope you will enjoy the party very much indeed."

"And what have you to say of me?" asked her father, presenting himself before her.

"That I'm very proud of my handsome papa," she answered, ending a hasty survey of his whole person with a look of love and delight up into his face as he stood gazing fondly down upon her.

"Love makes my little girl blind to any imperfection in her father," he said, taking her in his arms for a moment's caressing before he bade her good night. "Now, go to sleep," he said as he laid her down and tucked the covers carefully about her.

The next afternoon, Mr. Dinsmore and the two ladies, feeling the need of rest and sleep—for they had returned very late from the party—each indulged in a nap.

Elsie, who was not sleepy, thought the house had never before seemed so quiet and lonely. She missed Annis more than she had on any previous day. She would have gone out for a walk, but a steady rain forced her to remain indoors.

She wandered slowly, aimlessly, and with noiseless footsteps from room to room. At length entering her father's study, she seated herself in the chair he had occupied not long before beside his writing desk.

A book, a copy of *Oliver Twist*, lay open upon the desk, and as her eye fell on the printed page, she read at a glance enough to arouse within her an absorbing interest in its contents. Never stopping to look at the title or to consider whether it was such a work as she would be permitted to examine, she read on, hastily and eagerly, to the bottom of the page, turned it quickly, and perused the next and the next. She was so intensely interested as to be utterly oblivious of everything but the story, until a slight sound caused her to look up. She found her father standing close at her side, regarding her with a countenance of mingled astonishment and grieved, stern displeasure.

Instantly, her eyes fell beneath his gaze, while her face crimsoned with shame and embarrassment.

He gently took the book from her and, pointing to a large easy chair on the farther side of the room, said, "Sit there till I have time to attend to you."

His tone was very grave and sad, and she heard

him sigh deeply as she hastily and silently obeyed.

He paced the floor for some minutes, then seated himself at the desk, and for the next half-hour the room seemed painfully still. The slight scratching of his pen and an occasional half-stifled sob from Elsie were the only sounds save the ceaseless patter of the rain outside.

The child's tender conscience reproached her bitterly, and the loving little heart ached with a heavy burden of remorse because of the pain she had given to her almost idolized father.

"Oh, could it be possible that she had been guilty of such disobedience to so kind and dear a father—a father whose dear delight it was to heap favors and caresses upon her? How could she so wound him!"

And worse than all was the disobedience to her heavenly Father, whose command, 'Children, obey your parents,' she knew so well and had thought she loved to keep. Silently, and with bitter, repentant tears, she confessed her sin to Him and asked to be forgiven for Jesus' sake.

But she dared not address her earthly father until he should first speak to her. She trembled with fear of the punishment he might inflict. What would it be? Would he visit her transgression with the rod? She thought it not unlikely, for she felt that she deserved that and more. Oh, how dreadful if, in addition, he should deny her for days and weeks the seat upon his knee, which was one of her dearest privileges, the caresses and tender, loving words she so reveled in! How could she bear it?

The time of waiting for his verdict seemed very long. Would it ever come to an end? And yet, when at last he laid aside his pen and turned in her direction, she trembled and shrank from the ordeal that was before her.

"Elsie!" His tone was very grave and stern.

"Sir!" she answered with a voice full of tears.

"Come here to me!"

She obeyed instantly.

"Oh, father! Papa!" she sobbed, falling on her knees at his feet, "I've been a very wicked, disobedient child! I deserve to be severely punished, but I—" She could not go on for the sobs that were nearly choking her.

He lifted her gently and drew her to him. "I cannot tell you," he said in moved tone, "how deeply, how sorely, I am pained to find that I cannot trust my daughter, the dear darling of my heart, as I fondly believed I could! To find that she is but an eye-servant, obeying me carefully in my presence but disobeying my most express commands when she thinks I shall not know it."

"Oh, papa!" she cried in a voice of anguish, hiding her face on his breast while her whole frame shook with bitter, bursting sobs. "I'd rather you would give me the severest whipping than say that! Oh, please believe that it is the very first time I ever did such a thing! You know all about every time I've disobeyed you."

"I do believe it," he answered. "I have never had reason to doubt my daughter's word."

She lifted her face and looked up gratefully, though humbly, through the tears.

"I am unutterably thankful to be able to say that," he went on. "And I am inclined to be the more lenient toward you because I feel that I am partly to blame for leaving temptation in your way, especially after allowing you to hear enough about these stories of Dickens's to greatly excite your curiosity and interest. Therefore, the only punishment I shall inflict is a prohibition of your visits to this room in my absence from it. You may come in as freely as heretofore when I am here to see what you do, but at other times—until I see fit to remove the prohibition—you are not to cross the threshold."

Elsie's tears fell fast. She felt her father's prohibition keenly because it meant lack of trust in her, yet she could but acknowledge that it was a far lighter punishment than she had expected or deserved.

"Dear papa, you are very, very kind not to punish me more severely," she said as he lifted her face and tenderly wiped away her tears with his own fine, soft handkerchief. Then, catching sight of his face, she said, "Oh, papa, papa! Don't look so grieved and sad!" She clung about his neck, unleashing a fresh burst of sobs and tears.

"My child, I must look as I feel," he sighed, holding her close to his heart. "I cannot be other than sad after such a discovery as I have made today."

"Oh, all the pain ought to be mine!" she sobbed, "I ought to bear it all! I want to!"

"But you cannot," he said. "Let that thought deter you from all future acts of disobedience. Sin always brings sorrow and suffering, and that

seldom to the evildoer alone. Usually, the innocent suffer with the guilty."

"That is the very worst part of my punishment," she sobbed. "But, oh, won't you believe,
papa, that I am very, very sorry for having disobeyed you, and I do not intend ever to do so
again?"

"Yes, I do believe that, and in proof of it, I shall
not forbid you to go freely to the library, though
there are novels there, and they are not kept
under lock and key."

"I don't deserve it," she said very humbly and
gratefully. "Oh, papa, I don't know how I could
be so wickedly disobedient to such a dear, good,
kind father as you!"

"And to an infinitely better and kinder Father,"
he added, in low, reverent tones. "I would have
you more concerned because of your sin against
Him than against me."

As he talked on for several minutes in the same
strain, her distress became so great that he found
it necessary to try to comfort her with assurances
from God's word of His willingness to forgive
those who are truly penitent, and who come to
Him for pardon, pleading the merits and atoning
blood of his dear Son.

Opening the Bible, he read to her: "'If any may
sin, we have an advocate with the Father, Jesus
Christ the righteous, and He is the propitiation
for our sins.' 'I, even I, am He that blotteth out
thy transgressions for mine own sake, and will
not remember thy sins.'"

"Papa, pray for me," she pleaded amid her sobs

and tears. "Ask God to forgive my sins and take away all the evil that is in me."

And he did, kneeling with her, his arm around her, her head against his breast.

"Now, my darling," he said, as he drew her to his knee again, "be comforted, remembering that precious assurance of His word, 'If we confess our sins, He is faithful and just to forgive us our sins, and to cleanse us from all unrighteousness.'"

"Such sweet, comforting words, papa," she said. Then, after a moment's silence, she added, "I don't mean to try to excuse my wrongdoing, papa, but just to tell you how I happened to disobey you so. A mere glance at the open page interested me so greatly in the story that I thought of nothing else till you were there beside me."

"Want of thought has done a great deal of mischief in the world, my child," he intoned.

CHAPTER XXIV

I shall the effect of this good lesson keep,
As watchman to my heart.

—SHAKESPEARE

MR. TRAVILLA SPENT the evening at the Oaks, arriving shortly before tea and remaining until Elsie had gone to her rooms for the night. He noticed that his little friend was not her usual merry, happy self. Her sweet face bore traces of tears, and as he watched her furtively, he was sure that now and then her eyes filled and that she found it difficult to conceal her emotion. Once or twice, too, she slipped out of the room for a few moments, to recover control of her feelings, he thought.

She was very quiet, scarcely speaking at all, unless addressed, but clung to her father even more closely than usual, her eyes often seeking his with a wistful, pleading look, to which he responded with a gentle caress, while his manner toward her was full of grave tenderness.

"She has displeased him in some way (absurdly and most tyrannically strict as he is), and is morbidly remorseful for it," was the conclusion Mr. Travilla came to, and he longed to comfort her.

Elsie was disappointed that she had to go away for the night without a few last minutes alone with her father. But just as she was ready for bed, he came in, took her on his knee, assured her that he was now not in the least angry with her, and comforted her again with sweet and appropriate texts of Scripture, telling of God's willingness to forgive those who truly repent of sin.

"Yes, papa," she said with fast-falling tears. "I know Jesus has forgiven me, but it breaks my heart to think I could so dishonor Him! He says, 'If ye love me keep my commandments,' and I have failed today, and yet I do love him! I'm sure I do! And you, too, dear papa. Can you believe it, after I have disobeyed you so?" she asked, her arm about his neck and her eyes, dim with tears, gazing beseechingly into his.

"My darling, precious child, I haven't a doubt of it!" he said, folding her close to his heart. Then, laying her in her bed, he kissed her good night and left her to her slumber.

Mr. Dinsmore always kept his little daughter's secrets, even from Rose. He thought it quite unnecessary to tell of any trouble between himself and his child, and if Rose occasionally perceived that something was wrong between them, she made no remark and asked no question. She noticed it in no way except by redoubling her kindness to both.

She had made the same observation that Mr. Travilla had that evening and had drawn pretty nearly the same conclusion. Her husband had been displeased with his little girl, but there had been a reconciliation, and the child would soon recover her wonted cheerfulness and merriment.

Elsie did seem very much like her usual self the next morning, and when her lessons were done, she joined her mamma in the parlor, bringing some needlework with her.

Adelaide had concluded her visit to the Oaks, and she and her brother had left a few moments before to drive over to Roselands.

So, Rose and Elsie were alone together for a little while, but presently Mr. Travilla joined them. He and Rose fell into desultory chat, to which Elsie was an interested listener. The talk turned at length upon engravings, and Rose spoke of a small but very fine one, lately bought by her husband, which Mr. Travilla had not yet seen.

"I want you to look at it," Rose said. "Elsie, dear," she added, turning to her little stepdaughter, "will you run to your papa's study and bring me his portfolio? I think it is in that."

Elsie's face crimsoned, and she seemed greatly confused and embarrassed. "Mamma, I—I— please don't ask me to," she stammered, then burst into tears.

Rose was greatly surprised. "What is it, dear?" she asked, with tender concern.

"Papa—papa has—forbidden me to go there, except when—when he is present," sobbed the little girl, dropping her work to hide her blushing face in her hands.

"Then never mind, dear, I should not have asked if I had known that," Rose said, in an undertone full of sympathy and affection. "I shall go myself."

Excusing herself, she left the room.

He seemed scarcely to hear her excuse, so entirely was he taken up with pitying tenderness toward the weeping, mortified, embarrassed child.

"My dear little friend," he said, drawing near and softly touching the shining curls of the bowed head, "what can I do to help and comfort you?"

"You are very kind," she sobbed, "but no one can help me."

"I have some influence with your papa," he said, "and would gladly use it in your behalf, if — if your trouble is that you have angered or displeased him. But I know he loves you very, very dearly, and surely, whatever you may have done, he will forgive and take you back into favor, if you tell him you are sorry."

"Papa is not angry with me now," she said, wiping away her tears and looking up earnestly into her friend's face. "But," and again her face flushed and her eyes fell while the tears rolled down her cheeks, "oh, you would hardly believe how very, very naughty and disobedient I was yesterday!"

"No, I don't know how to believe it. But your papa is —"

He left the sentence unfinished, but Elsie knew intuitively his thought — that her father was very strict and severe, and with a sudden generous resolve to prove that he was not, she told Mr. Travilla the whole truth, though she was deeply ashamed to have him know of her wrongdoing.

"Oh, it is dreadful, to think my dear father can't trust me!" she sobbed in conclusion. "But, you see, he was not severe with me, Mr. Travilla. If he had given me a hard whipping besides, it wouldn't have been any more than I deserved."

"A delicate, dear little girl like you!" he exclaimed. "I should never have respected him again if he had." But the last words were spoken so low and indistinctly that Elsie did not catch them.

"A very bad, disobedient little girl, Mr. Travilla," she sighed. "Oh, I couldn't have believed I ever would disobey papa so!"

"Do you know," he said gently, "your remorse seems to me altogether out of proportion to the offense—just reading a little in a forbidden book. Why, as a boy I was often guilty of far worse deeds, yet I thought myself rather a good sort of fellow after all."

Elsie understood this remark as merely an effort to comfort her by making light of her wrongdoing, and she answered it with a grateful look.

"Now, my dear, I wouldn't fret about it any more," he said, smoothing her hair with gentle, caressing hand. "I feel sure your papa will soon trust you as fully as ever. I should at this moment trust you to any extent, and I assure you I think you the best little girl I ever knew."

Elsie looked up in incredulous surprise. "You are very, very kind, sir! But papa does not think so; he knows me better." And another tear rolled quickly down her cheek.

"I hope," Mr. Travilla said, meditatively, "he won't think it necessary to deny you the promised visit to Ion because of this."

"I did not know about that," she said. "I thought our holidays were to be over when Annis returns."

"Yes, but we had arranged that you were to bring your books with you, spend the mornings at your tasks, and enjoy, for the rest of the day, whatever pleasures my mother and I might be able to provide. I think we could make it pleasant for you."

"Oh, I am sure of it, and I should like to go so much!" she said. "But I don't think papa will let me, and I am sure I do not deserve that he should."

"Well, we won't despair," he said cheerfully. "I know he doesn't allow any coaxing from you, but that is not forbidden to me, and if necessary, I shall try my powers of persuasion."

A call to the nursery had detained Rose, thus giving them time for this little talk, but now she was returning. They heard her light step coming down the hall, her voice and that of old Mr. Dinsmore in conversation.

"Grandpa! Oh, please excuse me, Mr. Travilla! I don't want him to see that—that—I've been crying," Elsie exclaimed and slipped out of the room by one door as they entered by another.

Her eyes were so full of tears that she did not see her father was near until he had her in his arms.

"What is the matter?" he asked tenderly.

Her answer was a fresh burst of tears and sobs.

They were near the door of her boudoir. He took her hand, led her in there, sat down on a sofa and drew her to his knee.

"Tell me what ails you," he said, and she knew by his tone that he would have the whole story. There was no escape for her, though, indeed, she was now and always ready enough to pour out all her griefs into his sympathizing ear.

So she told of her mamma's request and the confession it had forced from her, that she was forbidden to go to his study in his absence. She ended with, "Oh, papa, please, please remove the prohibition and punish me some other way! Won't you, dear papa?"

"What other way?"

"I don't know,"she answered, hiding her face on his shoulder.

"Shall I lock you up for a week on bread and water?"

"Oh, no, no! That would be worse! Everybody would know I had been very naughty. But I—I believe I'd almost rather you—would whip me, for nobody need know about it, and it would be all over in a few minutes."

"I shall not do that," he said very decidedly and in a moved tone, pressing her closer to his breast and touching his lips to her cheek. "How could I? You must bear the punishment I have decreed, but you shall have no other, and I hope it will not be long before I can trust you as fully as ever."

"Papa, can't you do it now?" she asked imploringly. "Won't you remove your prohibition?"

"No, now now, not for days or weeks."

Then she wept very bitterly.

"My little daughter," he said, tenderly wiping away her tears and smoothing the hair back from her heated brow, "I am very, very sorry for you, but do you feel so sure of your strength to resist the temptation before which you fell yesterday that you wish me to expose you to it again?"

"No, papa, oh, no!" she said with a look of new

comprehension in the eyes she lifted to his. "But is that why you refuse?"

"Yes, daughter, for I have not the least doubt that you fully intend to be obedient to me at all times, whether I am present or absent."

"Oh, papa, thank you! Thank you very much!" she said, putting her arms about his neck while her face grew almost bright. "I thought your prohibition meant doubt that I intended to be good and obedient, but now I don't want it removed, because—because I—am not sure I could withstand temptation," she added, humbly, a vivid blush suffusing her face.

That evening Mr. Dinsmore told Elsie of the intended visit to Ion, adding that it was to be made the next week.

"And will you let me go after I have been so naughty, papa?" she asked, in glad surprise.

"Have I ever punished you twice for the same fault?" he inquired.

"No, sir, oh, no!"

"Then why should you expect it in this instance?"

"I don't know, papa, only that I—I feel that I am so very, very undeserving of such a pleasure," she murmured, hanging her head and blushing painfully.

"That question is not under consideration," he said, gently lifting the downcast face so that he might kiss the sweet lips again and again. "We all have very many blessings that we do not deserve."

CHAPTER XXV

The mountain rill
Seeks with no surer flow the far, bright sea,
Than my unchanged affections flow to thee.

— PARK BENJAMIN

THE LANDRETHS AND Annis returned to the Oaks on Monday of the next week, and on Tuesday all went to Ion, where the rest of the week was spent most delightfully.

There was a large dinner party the first day, but after that, they were the only guests, and their host and hostess quite laid themselves out for their entertainment.

Rose and Mildred enjoyed many a nice, quiet chat with Mrs. Travilla in the mornings while the little girls were busy with their tasks. The afternoons, when the weather permitted, were spent in the open air, walking, riding, or driving. In the evenings, all gathered about the fire, and lively conversation, enigmas, stories, games, and music made the time fly so fast that the little folks could scarcely believe the clock was right when it told them their hour for going to bed had come.

Annis would sometimes have lingered if Elsie might have done so, too, but that Mr. Dinsmore would not allow. So, with a pleasant good night to all, they went away together, for they shared the same room and enjoyed it greatly.

On Saturday evening, they returned to the Oaks, and on Monday, the old round of duties and pleasures was taken up again.

One stormy afternoon, as the little girls sat together in Elsie's dressing room pleasantly busied in millinery and mantuamaking for the family of dolls, Annis said, "I read *Oliver Twist* while we were at Holly Hall."

Elsie looked up in surprise. "Did you? Would your father and mother let you read such books?"

"Well," returned Annis, blushing, "I never heard them mention *Oliver Twist* at all, and I peeped into it one day and found it so interesting I just couldn't help going on and reading the whole story. I thought, why shouldn't I read what Milly and Brother Charlie and Cousin Horace and Cousin Rose do?"

"Papa says," returned Elsie slowly, "that I might as well ask why the baby may not eat everything that we older ones do."

"I suppose he means that our minds haven't cut their teeth yet," said Annis. "But don't you wish you were grown up enough to read novels?"

"I don't know. I'd like to read them dearly well, but I love to be papa's little girl and sit on his knee."

"You'll do that when you're grown up," remarked Annis with a wise nod of her pretty head. "I'll tell you the story of *Oliver Twist* if you want me to."

The offer was a tempting one, Elsie did want so very much to know what became of Oliver finally, and all about several of the other characters in whom she had become interested. For one minute she hesitated, then said firmly, "It wouldn't be right for me to hear it, Annis dear, without papa's leave, and that I shouldn't even dare to ask. But I thank you all the same."

"Elsie, you are so good and obedient that you often make me feel ashamed of myself," Annis said with a look of hearty, affectionate admiration into her cousin's face.

The fair face crimsoned. "No, no, Annis, I am not! Indeed I am not!" she exclaimed in tremulous tones, the tears springing to her eyes.

"Oh, I know you're a hypocrite and only pretend to be good!" returned Annis laughingly. "But there, I hear Milly calling me," she said, and hastily laying aside her work, away she ran.

"I wonder if I ought to tell her?" Elsie said to herself, wiping away a tear. "Oh, I don't want her to know! But I'm afraid it isn't right to let her think me so much better than I am."

Just then there was a gentle tap at the door leading into her boudoir. She rose quickly and opened it.

"Oh, Mr. Travilla! I am glad to see you, sir!" she said, offering her hand.

He took it and lifted it gallantly to his lips.

"Excuse me for coming in without an invitation, my little friend," he said. "I knocked at the other door, but no one seemed to hear, so I came on to this one."

"Please always feel free to do so, Mr. Travilla," she answered. "I think you have almost as much right as papa. Won't you take this easy chair?"

"Thank you, my dear," he said, accepting the invitation. "And now, if you will allow me another of your papa's privileges—that of taking you on my knee—you will make me very happy."

"Am I not growing too large and heavy, sir?" she asked, passively submitting to his will.

"No, not at all. I only wish you belonged to me so that I could have you here every day."

"Mr. Travilla, I thought you would never think well of me again, never love me anymore, after you learned how very naughty I was one day a few weeks ago," she murmured, blushing and hanging her head.

"My dear little girl," he said, stroking her hair, "that did not lessen my good opinion of you. On the contrary, your sorrow for what seemed to me but a slight misdemeanor, and your frank confession of it, raised you in my esteem, if that were possible, for I have long thought you very nearly perfect."

She shook her head, the blush deepening on her cheek. "Ah, sir, you make me feel like a hypocrite! And Annis has been talking so, too, and I—"

She hesitated, a troubled, anxious look on her sweet, innocent face.

"What is it, dear child?" he asked. "Anything I can help you with?"

"I was wondering if—if I ought to tell Annis about my—my naughtiness that day."

"I am quite sure you are under no obligation to

do so," he said, "and perhaps it would be better not to tell her."

Elsie looked relieved.

"Ah," he exclaimed, drawing something from his pocket, "I am forgetting the particular errand on which I came. Here is a book that you will enjoy, I think—and with your father's approval, for I submitted it to him before bringing it to you."

Elsie accepted the gift with warm thanks and looks of delight which well repaid him for his thoughtful kindness.

Annis came back presently, and after a little chat with her, Mr. Travilla left them to enjoy the book together.

Mr. Dinsmore's prohibition had not been removed, and Elsie still felt it keenly, though, while carefully observing it, she said nothing on the subject to her papa or anyone else.

One morning, she and Annis came in from a walk about the grounds, and while Annis went on into the house, Elsie lingered on the veranda, petting and playing with a favorite dog.

Looking round at the sound of horse's hoofs on the drive, she saw Dr. Landreth just reining in his steed at the foot of the veranda steps. The day being quite cold, there was no servant just at hand, though usually several could be seen lounging near this, the principal entrance to the mansion, so he called to her.

"Elsie, my dear, I have ridden back from the gate to recover my notebook, which I think I must have left on the table in your father's study. Will you run and get it for me?"

Elsie felt her cheeks grow hot. What should she do? She was almost certain her father was not in the house. Must she explain to the doctor why she could not go into his study when he was not there? No, she would summon a servant to do the errand, though that would take longer than to do it herself, and the doctor seemed in haste and would wonder and probably be vexed at the delay. But it could not be helped. She dared not, would not disobey her father. All this passed through her mind in an instant.

"I will get it as quickly as I can, sir," she said and hurried into the house.

She rapped lightly on the study door, then opened it and peeped in. It was just possible her papa might be there.

Yes, oh, joy! There he was, sitting by the fire reading the morning paper, and looking up from it, he said pleasantly, "I am here. Come in, daughter."

"The doctor sent me for his notebook papa," she said, glancing about in search of it.

"Yes, there it is on my writing desk."

"May I come back when I have given it to him, papa?" she asked as she took it up and turned to go.

"Yes, you may always come in when I am here. Your father loves to have you with him."

There was a flash of joy in the beautiful eyes looking into his, and the doctor thought, as he took the notebook from her hand, that he had never seen a brighter, happier face.

"Many thanks, my dear," he said, lifting his hat with a bow and smile, then turned his horse's head and galloped away.

Elsie looked after him for a moment, then hastened back to her father.

He greeted her entrance with a smile full of fatherly love and pride.

"Take off your hat and cloak," he said, "and ring for a servant to carry them away."

She did so, then came and stood close at his side, putting her arm around his neck and laying her cheek to his.

"My papa! My own dear, dear papa!" she murmured lovingly.

"My precious little daughter!" he responded, laying down his paper and drawing her to his knee. I thought I saw a cloud on my darling's face as she peeped in at the door yonder a few moments earlier. What troubled you, dearest? Tell papa all about it."

"I was afraid you were not here, and so I couldn't come in to do the doctor's errand. And I didn't want to tell him so; I didn't want him to know why. It does seem, father, as if I'm in danger of having everybody find out about my naughtiness and—and my punishment," she said, blushing and hanging her head, the troubled look again on her face.

He did not answer immediately but sat for some minutes silently caressing her hair and cheek. Then he said in low, tender accents, "My little girl, I think I may fully trust you now. I remove the prohibition and give you full permission to come in here when you will as freely as ever."

"Dear, papa, thank you! Oh, thank you very

much!" she cried joyfully, repaying him with the sweetest kisses and smiles.

"Do you love me very much? he asked.

"Oh, more than tongue can tell! I always did, always shall. I'm sure, sure I can never love anybody else half so dearly!"

"Suppose I should again become as cold, stern, and severe to my little girl as I once was?" he asked with a tremor of pain and remorse in his tones and pressing her close to his heart as he spoke.

"I should love you still, papa," she answered, tightening her clasp of his neck and showering kisses on his face. "But, oh, don't ever be so! It would break my heart if you should quit caressing me and not let me sit here and hug and kiss you."

"Don't fear it, my precious one," he said with emotion. "You could scarcely suffer more than I from a cessation of these sweet love passages between us."

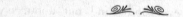

CHAPTER XXVI

'Mid pleasures and palaces though I may roam,
Be it ever so humble, there's no place like no home.

WINTER SPED RAPIDLY away to our friends at the Oaks, each day so full of agreeable, useful employment and quiet pleasures that they found it all too short. Time never hung heavy on their hands; ennui was unknown to them.

No unusual or startling event marked the course of the weeks and months. Mildred and Annis kept up a steady correspondence with mother and sisters, and now and then the letters from Pleasant Plains seemed to bring with them a touch of homesickness. But it would pass off directly, leaving the victims as lighthearted and happy as before.

And so it continued until spring had set in and they knew that April suns and showers were bringing out buds and leaves and waking flowers in garden and woods even in their northern home. Then, in spite of a very strong affection for these relatives and kind entertainers, and a very sincere regret at the thought of parting from them, they were seized with an unquenchable desire for home—home and mother. They longed for all the dear ones, but mother most of all.

The business affair which had called Dr. Landreth south had now been brought to a prosperous issue, and as there was no longer any necessity for remaining, an early date was set for their departure.

The doctor and his wife, conversing together in the privacy of their own apartments one bright sunshiny morning, had just settled this question when Annis came running in.

Mildred, with the brightest, happiest face she had worn for days, was dandling little Percy on her knee, telling him between rapturous kisses, "He shall go home to dear grandpa and grandma, so he shall, the darling babe!"

"Oh, Milly, are we going home soon?" cried Annis breathlessly.

"Yes, next week, your brother says."

"If you think you can be ready by that time," added the doctor.

"I!" exclaimed Annis. "I'd be ready in an hour if you and Milly would. Oh, I'm so glad, so glad! I must run and tell Elsie."

"And don't you hope she will be as glad as you are?" asked the doctor jokingly.

"Oh, it will be hard to leave Elsie!" she said, stopping short and with a look of distress. "I wonder if we couldn't persuade Cousin Horace to let us take her along to spend the summer at our house."

"Try it, Annis. There's nothing like trying," remarked the doctor with mock gravity. "But I advise you to extend your invitation to him or, better still, to the whole family. You'll have more chance of success."

"I wish they would all go with us," Mildred said.

"So do I, my dear, but I know that it wouldn't suit Dinsmore to be absent from the plantation just at present."

"Then why did you advise me to invite him?" asked Annis in a piqued tone.

"Because, in my opinion, one might as well ask for the gift of his entire fortune as for leave to carry his little girl so far from him."

"Oh, Brother Charlie, didn't father and mother let me come just as far away from them? And to stay away just as long?"

"Really, I had not thought of that!" laughed the doctor. "Well, ask Mr. Dinsmore, but if he says no, make allowance for the fact that he has but one daughter, while your father and mother rejoice in a goodly number."

"I'll go and do it this minute!" she exclaimed with energy and determination. "But first, I'll invite them all, shan't I, Milly?" she asked, looking back from the doorway.

"Yes, tell them nothing could give greater pleasure to us or mother and the rest at home."

Running lightly down the broad stairway into the spacious hall below, Annis heard a sound of cheerful voices, mingled with peals of merry child laughter, coming from the veranda beyond.

The air was warm and balmy with the breath of flowers, and doors and windows stood open, giving to the passerby delightful glimpses of the grounds lovely with the verdure and bloom of spring.

From the veranda, the view was more extended, and there the whole family had taken themselves for the full enjoyment of it. Here Annis found them, Mr. and Mrs. Dinsmore sitting side by side, little Horace on his father's knee, and Elsie romping with him, laughing merrily herself and making him laugh while the parents looked on with pleased and happy faces.

"Ah, Annis, will you come and join us?" Mr. Dinsmore said, catching sight of the little girl as she stepped from the open doorway.

"Thank you, Cousin Horace," she returned, coming forward in eager haste. "I have some news to tell."

"Ah! Then let us have it."

Elsie stopped her romping, stood still, and turned to listen.

"It is that we are to start for home next week, and, oh, Cousin Horace, we want to take you all with us!" she said, ending with Mildred's message.

The expression of Elsie's face changed rapidly as Annis spoke. At first, it was full of regret at the prospect of losing her cousins' companionship, then of pleasure at the thought of going with them.

"Oh, papa, can we?" she asked eagerly.

"No, daughter, it would not suit me to leave home at present. But we all thank you and Mildred very much for your kind invitation," he added to Annis, "and are very sorry to hear that we are to lose you so soon."

"Yes, Annis. Ah, what shall I do without you!" exclaimed Elsie.

"Cousin Horace, I wish you could go," said Annis. "But if you can't, you will let Cousin Rose and little Horace and Elsie go, won't you?"

"My dear," he said, turning to his wife, "how would you like to go as far as Philadelphia with them? Your mother has been very urgent of late for a visit from you and the boy," he said with a fatherly, smiling glance at his little son, "and this would be an excellent opportunity."

"I should so much prefer to have you with me," Rose answered with hesitation.

"If you want to make a long visit, your wisest course will be to go without me," he returned with a smile. "I will follow some weeks later and bring you home."

"I must take time to think of it," she said. "And Elsie? You will let me take her with me?"

"And let her go on with us?" put in Annis.

"I am inclined to think I should not risk much in leaving the decision of both questions with her," he said with a tenderly affectionate glance into the sweet face of his little girl.

"Leave you, papa! To go so far away and stay so long?" she exclaimed, springing to his side and clasping her arms tight about his neck. "Oh, no, no, no! Never—unless you make me do it!"

"Make you!" he said, holding her close to his heart with a low, happy laugh. "I don't know what could induce me to permit it. My wife's parents have some claim on her and their little grandson," he added, looking fondly at Rose, "but you, daughter, belong entirely to me, and here you must stay while I do."

She heard his verdict with a gleeful laugh, gave him a long hug and kiss, then turned to Annis and put her arms about her. "Oh, Annis, dear!" she said in tremulous tones, the tears filling her eyes. "What shall I do without you?"

"Look forward to another happy time together at some future date," suggested Mr. Dinsmore cheerily. "And now, if you will don your riding habits, we will have a gallop. I have ordered the ponies and a horse for myself, and they will be here very shortly."

The little girls were both very fond of riding, and smiles banished tears from their faces as they hastened to do his bidding.

He exerted himself, and with good success, through the few remaining days of Annis's stay, to keep them so busily and pleasantly employed that there should be little time for the indulgence of vain regrets.

Rose was not long in deciding to avail herself of this good opportunity to visit her parents, and as they made their preparations for the journey, the heart of each proud young mother was full of fond anticipation of the delight she should feel in showing her lovely baby boy to his grandparents, aunts, and uncles.

"They will hardly know Percy at home, he has grown and improved so much!" Mildred said to her husband.

"Very much indeed! Yet I think they will not be long in doubt of his identity," the doctor responded with a proud, loving glance from wife to son and back again. "He has his mother's eyes and smile."

When the appointed day came, it found all in readiness for the journey.

Mr. Dinsmore and Elsie accompanied the travellers to the city, saw them on board the train, and took leave of them there.

"Oh, papa!" Elsie said, sobbing on his breast as they drove homeward, "partings are so dreadful—partings from those you love and don't expect to see again for a long, long while!"

"Yes, darling, I feel them to be so myself, and I know it must be harder still for a little one like you with such a loving, tender heart," he answered, soothing her with caresses.

"How selfish I am, dear papa!" she exclaimed, lifting her head to look into his face and noting its sad expression. "How thoughtless I am to forget how hard it must be for you to see mamma and little brother go away."

"Selfishness is quite foreign to your nature, I think, dear daughter," he said. "And though I do feel keenly the parting from those dear ones, the weeks of separation cannot look nearly so long to me as they do to one of your age. But we will look forward to the happy meeting we hope for at the end of those weeks. And we have each other still," he added with a cheery smile. "Should not that be enough to make us at least tolerably happy?"

"Oh, yes, dear papa! How much worse to be parted from you than from all the rest of the world! I will not cry anymore," she said with determination, wiping away her tears and smiling sweetly into the eyes that were gazing so fondly into hers.

She kept her word, exerting herself to be cheerful and to win her father from sad thoughts by loving caresses and sweet, innocent prattle.

He seconded her efforts, and before they reached home, they were laughing and jesting right merrily.

But as they crossed the threshold, she said with quivering lip and tremulous voice, "Papa, how very lonely it seems! And it will be still more so in my own room without Annis and away from you."

"Then suppose you spend all your time with me."

"Oh, may I!" she asked, looking up delightedly into his face.

"Every moment from the time you are dressed in the morning till your retire at night. That is, if you wish it and can contrive to learn your lessons by my side in the hours when I am indoors. In that case, you may go with me when and wherever I go."

"Oh, how nice, dear papa!" she cried, clapping her hands and dancing about in her delight.

"Yes," he said, sitting down and taking her in his arms to caress her. "I think we shall be very happy together even without anyone to help us enjoy ourselves. We were in former days, were we not, darling?"

"Yes indeed, papa! When we first came to this sweet home, and each of us was all the other had. Let us pretend we've gone back to those old times just for a little while. Wouldn't it be a nice variety?"

"It seemed a very nice variety then, and you may pretend it as strongly as you please," he said with an amused, indulgent smile.

THE END

The Original Elsie Classics

Elsie Dinsmore

Elsie's Holidays at Roselands

Elsie's Girlhood

Elsie's Womanhood

Elsie's Motherhood

Elsie's Children

Elsie's Widowhood

Grandmother Elsie

Elsie's New Relations

Elsie at Nantucket

The Two Elsies

Elsie's Kith and Kin

Elsie's Friends at Woodburn

Christmas with Grandma Elsie

Elsie and the Raymonds

Elsie Yachting with the Raymonds

Elsie's Vacation

Elsie at Viamede

Elsie at Ion

Elsie at the World's Fair

Elsie's Journey on Inland Waters

Elsie at Home

Elsie on the Hudson

Elsie in the South

Elsie's Young Folks

Elsie's Winter Trip

Elsie and Her Loved Ones

Elsie and Her Namesakes

6/19